# BEGGING FOR CHANGE

# Also by Sharon G. Flake

*The Skin I'm In*

*Bang!*

*Who Am I Without Him?*

*You Don't Even Know Me*

*Money Hungry*

# BEGGING FOR CHANGE

## SEQUEL TO *MONEY HUNGRY*

## SHARON G. FLAKE

Disney Jump at the Sun
Los Angeles New York

Copyright © 2003 by Sharon G. Flake

All rights reserved. Published by Disney • Jump at the Sun, an imprint of Disney Book Group. No part of this book may be reproduced or transmitted in any form or by any means, electronic or mechanical, including photocopying, recording, or by any information storage and retrieval system, without written permission from the publisher. For information address Disney • Jump at the Sun, 125 West End Avenue, New York, New York 10023.

First Hardcover Edition, June 2003
First Paperback Edition, July 2004

10 9 8 7 6 5 4 3 2 1

FAC-025438-18355

Printed in the United States of America

This book is set in 12-point Janson Text LT Pro/Fontspring

Library of Congress Control Number for Hardcover: 2003536687

ISBN 978-1-368-01941-5

Visit www.DisneyBooks.com

*For Myra Kim Smith Flake, who blessed us
with love, laughter, and a well-lived life.
You are much missed.
And
for Garen Thomas, my editor.
You are GOOD,
very, very good. . . .
Thanks much for all you've done.*

# CHAPTER ONE

THEY NEVER CALL ME OVER the intercom at school.

But I can tell by the way the secretary is saying my name over that thing—I'm in trouble.

"Raspberry Hill," she says real slow, with a crack in her voice. "Come, come to the office, please."

Kids start teasing me. Saying I must be in *big* trouble. On my way outta English class, one girl looks at me and says, "You lucky. You probably get to go home for doing something stupid. Wish it was me."

No way would that girl wanna be me right now, sitting in the hospital hoping my mother don't die. Mad at God and everyone else who shoulda looked out for her, but didn't.

In school, there ain't never a good reason to cry.

If you accidentally cut your hand off in wood shop, you better hold back them tears. 'Cause if you let 'em loose, somebody gonna say you a punk, and you won't never live that down. But it's okay to cry in this place. And that's just what I do. I cry all the while I'm in the waiting room. Cry some more when I see how really bad off Momma is.

The newscaster on the TV in the hospital waiting room said Momma was jumped in broad daylight right out front of our place. Wasn't no stranger who whacked her over the head, neither. It was Shiketa Nixon, the girl who lives two buildings up from us. She's seventeen, but she looks twenty-five. And she don't know nothing 'bout picking up her own mess, or telling her no-good friends to stop waking up the whole neighborhood at three and four in the morning with loud music, crap games, and fights.

Momma called the cops on Shiketa three times last week. Called the fire department once too when one of Shiketa's friends set an old mattress on fire just for fun.

I told Momma to leave that girl be. But you know Momma. She can't leave good enough alone. This morning she said she was gonna have another talk with Shiketa. And she wasn't gonna be nice about it neither. I guess Shiketa had enough of Momma. The newscaster said she took a metal pipe to her head. Right in front of everybody.

When the evening nurse comes on duty, she thumps the IV line running from the clear plastic bag right into Momma's smooth, brown arm. Then she frowns at the patch of missing hair they shaved from Momma's head so they could stitch up the hole that Shiketa put there. I hold my breath when she wipes the blood away and puts a new bandage on.

"Excuse me," I say, making a run for the bathroom. Flushing the toilet so the nurse don't hear me throwing up the pudding and creamed chicken they left Momma earlier, even though a blind man could see she can't eat nothing.

"You all right, honey?" the nurse says, knocking on the door.

I wipe my mouth with the back of my hand. "Yeah."

Through the closed door, I hear the nurse trying to wake Momma up. They do that every hour to make sure she's okay. That she ain't in a coma or hemorrhaging on the brain. Momma tells the nurse her name, address, and the day of the week. I crack open the bathroom door, walk over to the bed.

"My head hurts," Momma says, reaching for my hand. Yawning. Turning her back on me and the nurse and going back to sleep.

The nurse's voice feels like a warm washcloth on my face. "My shift is just about over, honey. I'll see you tomorrow, okay?"

I nod my head up and down.

"Can I call somebody for you? You too young to be here by yourself," she says, pulling the covers up over Momma.

I tell the nurse that I ain't here by myself. My girlfriend Zora and her dad are with me. He's a doctor. I called him when the school said something bad happened to Momma. He closed down his practice for the day. Picked me and Zora up and drove us here. Zora went to the gift shop to buy me some tissues. "Nice ones. Not the cheap, rough ones they have here," she said, pointing to a tissue box in Momma's room. That was an hour and fifteen minutes ago.

"You take care, okay? Your momma looks bad, but the doctors say she'll be all right," the nurse says, walking out.

I lay down beside Momma. Stare at dry blood caked around the edge of her hair and the tip of her left ear. I wet a tissue. Drag it along her hairline. Wet it again and wipe her ear inside and out. I lean over to get a good look at her head again, then lay my head down and cry. That's why I don't see my father walk into the room. All I know is, something stinks real bad. When I lift my head up, there he is. Standing by the door.

"Raspberrrry," he says, dragging my name out like he did when I was little and he couldn't find me nowhere. His short red hair is knotty and matted to his head like it ain't been combed in months. He's wearing a T-shirt, ripped at the collar, that's got more dirt on it than Shiketa's front steps.

"Oh, Daddy," I say, squeezing Momma's fingers.

"Girl. Come give me a hug," he says, wiggling his lips, and poking 'em out, like I'm supposed to kiss him.

I shake my head from side to side, push the button by Momma's bed so the nurse will come. I'm sorry as soon as I do that, 'cause they just might throw Daddy out. Or lock him up. 'Cause anybody can see that he's drunk, maybe high on crack right now too.

Daddy's eyes are half open. And he can't stand still unless he's holding on to something, or sitting down on Momma's bed, like he's doing now.

"I saw the news. They said what happened to her," he says real low. "I was at McDonald's. Trying to come down, you know," he says. "Got ahold of some bad stuff. Been up for four days straight."

I buzz the nurse again. Cover my face with my hands. Pray to God that nothing happens to Momma, 'cause Daddy can't take care of hisself, let alone me.

"Somebody buzz?" the nurse says over the intercom. She sounds busy, like I'm interrupting her.

Daddy looks at me. His eyes are bloodshot, but I can still see the hurt in 'em.

"No," I say. "I sat on the buzzer. Accidentally."

Daddy smiles. Pushes the hair outta Momma's face. Takes a tissue and wets it with his spit and wipes something off her chin.

"It should be me here with my head bashed in," he says, rubbing her arm, then standing up, walking over to me, and asking if I need anything. "I got maybe five dollars in change," he says, digging into his pocket with one hand. Holding on to the bed with the other.

I look down at the floor. "No. I'm okay."

"Good," he says. "'Cause I ain't do so well on the corner today. Folks was cheap with their cash. You know sometimes it's like that," he says, walking over to the window and staring into the night. "Some days they make you beg for every penny they give you. Other times they throw a buck or two in your cup like they made of money."

After a while, Daddy and me ain't got nothing more to say. So I'm glad when Zora walks in the room. Only she don't see him at first, and before I can stop her she's holding her nose closed and saying, "It stinks in here!"

I don't say a word. I just point to where *he* is, and listen to Zora apologize over and over again. Daddy acts like she never said a word. But a few minutes later, he's at the door saying it's time for him to go.

"Give me some sugar, baby girl," he says, walking over to me, pressing his hard, dry lips to my cheek, and kissing me good-bye. Then he walks out the door, whistling and jingling change in his pocket, like he ain't got a care in the world.

# CHAPTER TWO

I DON'T WANT TO GO TO ZORA'S house tonight. I want to sleep in my own bed. That's what I tell her dad when he comes to check on Momma, and to take me and Zora back to their place for the night. But he ain't having it. So I kiss Momma good night. Get in the backseat of their car and slam the door shut.

When Dr. Mitchell's Lexus pulls outta the lot, I look out the back window. Check out the bums sitting on the curb and digging through trash bins in the alley across the street. Then I close my eyes, hoping I don't see Daddy.

It's hot out. But inside, I feel like the cold, crusty stuff you scrape off ice cream that's been in the freezer too long. I wanna cry, but I ain't got no more tears left.

"Want some air?" Dr. Mitchell asks, leaning over the seat and staring down at me.

"No," I say.

"Yeah. It's hot," Zora says, fanning herself.

The windows go up and the air comes on. "We'll compromise," her dad says, "and put the air on low."

I lie across the backseat. Put Dr. Mitchell's hospital jacket over my face and pretend I'm asleep, so nobody will try to talk to me.

"You all right, Raspberry?" he asks.

I keep my mouth closed.

"Raspberry?" he says again. "You all right back there?"

The words fly out my mouth. "Would you be all right," I say, with his jacket still covering my head, "if your mother got hit in the head with a pipe and your father was high as a kite?"

Dr. Mitchell takes his time answering.

"No. I guess I wouldn't," he says, stepping on the gas. "I'd be mad, sad, too. Just like you, sweetie."

I stick my fingers in my ears and tell myself not to listen to nothing Dr. Mitchell's saying, 'cause people like him ain't got no worries. They got big bucks and big houses. Nice rides and tight jobs. And then there's me and Momma. Bad luck and hard times is all we know.

"You want pizza?" Zora says, reaching back and pulling her father's jacket off my face.

I cover myself back up. "No."

She pulls the jacket off again. "I didn't eat all day. Just M&M's."

Dr. Mitchell says there's nothing cooked at their place. So we need to eat before we go home. "What about going through the drive-thru and picking up some chicken?"

I don't want chicken. I don't want pizza. I want my mother. But I keep that to myself, 'cause I don't want them thinking I'm being a baby. "Pizza," I say, covering myself up again. Wishing I could just go home.

Zora tells her dad to stop at the ATM machine too, 'cause tomorrow's the last day to pay on the class trip to Canada.

I dig in my pockets and pull out a ten-dollar bill and four quarters. Take my fingernails and run 'em all the way down the back of Dr. Mitchell's lemon yellow seats. *I was gonna go on the trip too*, I say to myself, *but I guess that ain't gonna happen.*

I don't say nothing to Zora and her dad when we get to the pizza shop. I don't even look at 'em. I stare down at the floor. Listen to the reporter on TV talk about what happened to Momma and ignore Dr. Mitchell when he says that it's a shame somebody as nice as her got hurt for trying to make the community better.

*Shut up!* I want to say. 'Cause he ain't *in* the community. He's in a really nice neighborhood where people like me and Momma ain't wanted. Where he don't have to worry 'bout people trying to knock his head off for doing the right thing.

"Say something," Zora says, blowing the wrapper off her straw right into my plate.

I look at her. Ball up the paper and flick it back. *Don't talk to me,* I say in my head. *Don't be so happy when I'm so sad inside.*

Soon as the pizza comes, Zora takes a sip of soda and excuses herself so she can go to the bathroom. "Watch my purse," she says.

Dr. Mitchell moves closer to me. Covers my hand with his and says his life wasn't much different from mine when he was growing up in the projects. "A neighbor went after my mother, too—with a knife. She had to get twenty-one stitches. But she made it through. Your mom will, too. I promise," he says, patting my cheek, then wolfing down his pizza.

I don't mind Dr. Mitchell telling me how things

were when he was young, 'cause I wanna be like him when I grow up. A doctor—or somebody that makes a whole lot of money.

The waitress refills the glasses. She smiles and asks Dr. Mitchell real nice if we want anything else. I wanna tell her to get up outta his face, 'cause that's my mother's man. When she's gone, I look at him myself. He's nice-looking. Tall and thin with thick curly black hair and my color skin—pretty brown with a lot of red to it. He ain't got no mustache or sideburns, and he always wears the same color pants—tan. Momma likes him a whole lot. Me too, most times.

"Excuse me, sweetie. I need to use the bathroom," he says, knocking Zora's purse on the floor when he gets up to go.

I throw the purse back in the seat. Pick gray sausage balls off my pizza and flick 'em onto Zora's plate and chair. The waitress walks by and asks if everything is okay with my food. Her eyes roll when she sees the mess I made. I give her a fake smile and reach for Zora's purse. I wipe the grease off and keep it in my lap while the waitress heads for another table.

The door to the men's room opens right when I pull back the thick, gold zipper on Zora's red purse. I swallow hard. Tell myself to put the purse back where

I got it. I don't. I feel around inside for cash when I see Dr. Mitchell ain't the one coming out. I take the money—a lot of it. Smell it. Put it away quick when the girls' room door opens. It's Zora. She's smiling at me from way across the room. My fingers shake. I almost drop the purse. By the time she and her dad get to the table, it's like nothing ever happened.

"Here," Dr. Mitchell says, putting eighty dollars down in front of me. Eighty more in front of Zora.

I look at him like he's crazy.

"For the class trip," he says. "You're going, right? The money's due tomorrow."

My feet itch from the money I put in my sock. And my heart hurts. But I ain't sure if it's from the greasy sausage pizza, or 'cause I know how sad Momma would be if she saw what I just did.

"Take it," Zora says, handing me half the money, and putting the rest in her purse.

I take the money. Crumple it up like used tissue and stuff it deep, down in my pocket. I don't look at them the rest of the time we sit there. I pick the meat off the pizza. Smash the little balls with my thumb, and wonder what Zora's gonna think when she figures out what I done.

# CHAPTER THREE

**I** **PUT UP SUCH A FUSS** on the way back to the car that Dr. Mitchell gives in and takes me back to our place. He says I can't stay there alone, but I can grab a few things and make sure the place is all right.

Zora says none of this woulda happened if Momma and me had gotten that Section Eight house in Pecan Landings. Momma tried. But the neighbors went to court to keep us out. They think people living in Section Eight housing are poor, dirty, and bad for the neighborhood. We got a lawyer fighting for us to be able to move in there. But I ain't so sure that place will ever be ours.

There's like ten people on the steps of our apartment building when Dr. Mitchell drives up to our place. About six more on Shiketa's porch, smoking weed and drinking forties. They're acting like they're waiting for somebody or something. Dr. Mitchell presses a button and locks all the doors. Then clears his throat and says, "We'll come back for your things some other time."

I wrap my hand around the money he gave me, and think about the money I got stashed in our apartment. "You was raised in the projects, Dr. Mitchell. Don't you know how to fight?"

"You don't know how to fight yourself," Zora says.

She's right. But after all I been through today, I feel like I can beat the crap outta everybody in the whole wide world.

Dr. Mitchell's trying to prove he ain't no punk, I guess. He unlocks the door and gets out the car. "You two wait here," he says, locking us in.

I roll down the window. Lean out and listen to Shiketa's friends tell Dr. Mitchell he better get back in his ride if he know what's good for him. A tall girl wearing a burgundy weave way past her shoulders calls my name and heads for the car like we friends. Dr. Mitchell tries to keep his eyes on her and watch the other kids too. He tells the girl that I can't talk to nobody right now.

"I just wanna see her. Dag," she says, giving him the finger.

I seen her before. She's friends with Shiketa.

"Hey, Raspberry," she says, getting up in my face. Trying to sound like we best friends. "Tell your mother to chill and lay off Shiketa."

Zora and me don't say a word.

Weave Girl bangs her fist on the roof of the car. "You hear me, girl?"

"Everybody saw what Shiketa did," I say, checking out the girl's faded silver tongue ring when she opens her mouth to tell me off again.

"Your mother was always picking on her. So she got what she got," the girl says, ducking when a bottle smashes against the tire and glass flies everywhere.

Zora opens the door wide. "Daddy!" she yells. "Let's go!"

Something else hits the car, hard. Dr. Mitchell runs over to us. "Shut the windows. Lock the doors. Now!" he says, pulling open the trunk and heading back for my place with a big, black bat. "You hit her . . . with a pipe. And now you're threatening me and my kids?" he says, running after them.

It feels so *good* having Dr. Mitchell take up for me—like a real father should. But I can't think on that too long. Zora's dialing 911 on her dad's cell, trying to get us some help. "My dad's a cop. I mean, a doctor," she says, "and he needs help." She looks back at me and asks what my address is.

Kids are running all over the place. Some are laughing. Others cussing, saying what they gonna do to Dr. Mitchell if he touches them with that thing.

"Get 'em, Dr. Mitchell!" I yell. "Make 'em pay for what happened to Momma!"

Zora's blue eyes look clear and cold when she looks back at me. "It should be your father out here taking up for you and your mother. Not mine."

She's right. Her father should be home watching TV maybe, or doing bills, not out here ready to bust somebody's head open. "If the cops see your father with that bat, he's gonna get in trouble," I say, looking over at her dad.

Zora rolls down the window and begs her dad to get back in the car. I call him too. I tell him I don't need my stuff right now. I can get it later. Good thing, too. 'Cause ain't no way we're getting into my place tonight. Three big boys are chasing Dr. Mitchell back to the car.

"Get the windows up. Put your seat belts on," he

says, throwing the bat in the backseat with me, slamming the door shut.

Dr. Mitchell's ride makes a fast, crooked line up our street, rolling over the curb and running over a plastic trash can. The car is smooth and fast, and flies through the next three red lights like it's got wings instead of tires.

I lie across the backseat—with Dr. Mitchell's jacket covering my face—hoping the car never stops.

# CHAPTER FOUR

"**Y**OUR FAMILY IS CURSED," Ja'nae says, throwing the basketball at the hoop. Making a face when it bounces off the rim and rolls into the bushes. Her short, fat arms look funny. But she makes the shot the next time.

It's four days after Shiketa jacked Momma up. Momma's still in the hospital, so I don't want to hear all this stuff Ja'nae is talking. Zora knows that, I guess. She says for Ja'nae to be quiet and play. She's over by the fence polishing her toes. Ain't mentioned nothing yet 'bout missing no money.

We at our girl Mai's house. She ain't here. "She made a run with her dad to the market," her mother said, "for more chicken backs and collards."

Zora, Ja'nae, and me came to get Mai so we could

go by the hospital and see Momma. She's supposed to be getting a CAT scan this morning, so Dr. Mitchell said I shouldn't come down until noon. I wanted to go to the hospital by myself. But Ja'nae asked me what I wanted to do that for. "It'll be more fun with friends," she said. Like we was going to the movies or something.

Ja'nae dribbles the basketball, walking my way. When she does, I smell baby powder. "I mean it," she says, wiping sweat off her forehead with a sweet-smelling cotton ball. "Everything bad happens to you and your mom. Everything."

I smack the basketball out her hand. Run it up to the basket. Sink it in. "Now who's cursed?" I say, strutting my stuff like them NBA players do.

I shoulda kept my mouth shut. Now Zora is naming all the bad stuff that's happened to me and Momma over the last few years. "Your father went on dope. Then you two moved in with friends till they kicked y'all out," she says, putting down the polish. "You were homeless for a while, then you moved into the projects and were robbed," she says, wiggling her toes so they can dry faster. "Seems like a curse to me."

I tell her she don't need to talk. Her family got

problems, too. But when I go to bust on her, all I can say is her parents are divorced and her mother's always at their place butting in her dad's business. That's it. Nothing.

Ja'nae puts her two cents in. I yell at 'em both to shut up. Then I pick up my stuff and start to leave.

Mai's mom comes over and puts her arm around me. "Why are you two being so mean?" she says, pointing to them.

Zora looks up from her nails. "We didn't mean—"

"Make yourselves useful," her mom says. "Go help Mai and her dad with the bags. I just heard the car pull up to the front of the house."

Zora ain't trying to go help nobody do nothing, even though Mrs. Kim tells her again to get moving. But before Mrs. Kim can put her in check, Mai shows up. "Hey," she says, picking up the basketball and shooting.

Mrs. Kim's soft hands feel sweaty holding mine. "All the bags in?" she asks Mai.

Mai smacks the ball to the ground over and over again. "Dad's bringing 'em."

Her mom goes off, saying how lazy and inconsiderate Mai is. She gives Mai the same tired speech my mom gives me. "You only think about yourself. We should stop doing for you all together and then see how you like it."

Ja'nae ain't like the rest of us. She likes cleaning and helping out. Before Mai's mom even started speechifying, Ja'nae was in the kitchen unpacking food.

Mai's mom is the color of chocolate chips. She's African American. Her dad is Korean. Ja'nae likes to get him to talk the way they do in his country. So with the screen door open you can hear him saying the Korean names of the fruits, vegetables, and meat they're unpacking in there. Ja'nae repeats after him.

Mai's mom pushes open the door and goes inside. "Ungrateful," she says, talking about Mai.

I look at my watch and tell Zora and 'em that it's time to leave. "Momma should be back from getting her CAT scan now."

Mai picks up the ball and lays up another shot. When her sleeve rolls back, Zora and me go nuts.

"Oh my God. Oh my God," Zora says running over to Mai. "When did you do it?" she says, staring at the tattoo on Mai's arm.

In red and black swirls as tall as my baby finger, Mai's tattoo says 100% BLACK.

"I got it yesterday," she says, putting down the ball. Letting us get a good look at her arm. "Don't touch it. It still hurts."

The tattoo drilled into her skin is swelled up like wet paint after a rain. Mai blows on it, like she's trying to cool hot tea.

"My father went off when he saw it," she says, holding the ball still with her foot. "He says I branded myself, like a slave. Like he know something about that."

Zora's making a face, like she's looking at something disgusting. "My dad would kill me if I did that. He says it's not sanitary."

"My grandfather would cut my arm off and beat me over the head with it," Ja'nae says, walking up to us. "Anyhow, what you wrote on your arm ain't even true."

What'd Ja'nae say that for? Now she and Mai going at it. And Zora's putting in her two cents. Only I don't care about no stupid tattoo. I want to see my mother. Now! I tell 'em that too. But ain't nobody listening.

Mai gets up in Ja'nae's face. "You don't need to be talking about anybody else," she says, pointing to her hair. "That mess in your head ain't real neither."

She's talking about Ja'nae's new braids. "And neither are those blue contacts you got on, Zora."

Mai's eyes fix on me like she's trying to find something fake about me too. So I curl up my fingers to hide the nails I glued on at Zora's last night. Then Ja'nae says something else, and the three of 'em go at it again.

"Stop it!" I yell. They stare at me. I cover my face with my hands. "Please stop," I say, wishing somebody would have told that to Shiketa the day she went after Momma with that pipe.

# CHAPTER FIVE

**I** SMELL HIM EVEN BEFORE I set foot in Momma's room. He smells like stale corn chips and wet hair. I can't go in, not with my father there. So I lie to Mrs. Kim. Tell her I need to go to the gift shop to buy something special for my mother. Mrs. Kim goes into Momma's room all by herself. I go over to the stairwell across from the nurses' station, sit down, and hope my father's gone by the time I get back.

I wish my girls were here. But Mrs. Kim made Zora and Ja'nae go home and Mai stay in the house. "Raspberry needs peace and quiet at a time like this, not cackling hens pecking her to pieces," she said.

I sit on the top step. Check to see if anybody's coming before I pull off my sneakers and empty money into my lap. I take more cash out my pockets, lay all the bills down in a straight, neat row and count 'em—twice.

I got a hundred bucks on me. Woulda had more if I'd kept the money for the class trip. But I turned it in 'cause Dr. Mitchell's been real good to me, letting me stay at his place, buying me whatever I need. Somebody else woulda found my father and made *him* take care of me. Then where would I be? Living on the streets again. Begging for change.

Mrs. Kim comes to look for me after I've been gone half an hour. I follow her to the room. Ask her if she gonna stay till Momma comes. She says she won't leave me. I'm glad, 'cause when I get to the room, it's not just Daddy there. There's another man, too. He's lying on Momma's bed with all his clothes on. Even his shoes.

I stand statue still when Daddy walks over to me, kisses my cheek, and roughs up my face with his scratchy red beard. I lift my shoulder up and rub his kiss away.

The man on the bed opens one eye and stares up at me. Daddy introduces us. Tells the guy that he better leave before Momma comes back.

"Virginia never could stand no riffraff," Daddy

says, walking over to his friend. "She gonna go out her mind when she sees me here. Two bums might make her have a stroke," he says, laughing, like that's funny.

Mrs. Kim puts her big, warm arms around my shoulder.

"James," the man says with sleep in his voice. "You sure?"

Daddy paces the room. His light brown eyes jerk back and forth. His fingers pick at his face and arms, like he's pinching himself. "Yeah, I'm sure she ain't gonna want to see your sorry butt when she gets back," he says.

The man is outta the bed now, sitting down in a chair by the door. "I ain't talking about that," he says, pulling open a small dresser drawer. "There's plenty of clean washcloths here," he says holding one up. "Sure you don't want to take a hot shower?"

Daddy makes a sucking noise with his tongue. Then he takes ten sugar packs and empties 'em one by one into a cup of steaming hot tea. Snatches the washcloth out the guy's hand and goes into the bathroom. After a while, we hear the toilet flush. The shower going. A few minutes later, the room starts smelling like Ivory soap and cabbage.

The man is walking around the room, drinking Daddy's tea, asking us if we mind him taking a shower too. "Been a long time since we cleaned up good."

He don't wait for us to answer. He starts telling us how him and Daddy been friends since high school. "Who woulda thought," he says, shaking his head, "that we would end up on the streets together." He drinks up the last of the tea. Spoons out the thick, wet sugar from the bottom of the cup and eats it. "But it's all good," he says. "Somebody gotta have your back out there. To be your eyes while you sleep. To make sure you don't end up cut to pieces or dead as a doorknob."

"That's enough," Mrs. Kim says, pointing at the man. "The girl is only fourteen and her mother's in the hospital. Hurt. She doesn't need to hear all of this."

Daddy comes out the bathroom wearing the same old clothes. The dirt is gone from his face and hair, and the yellow crud caked between his teeth is not so bad now. *Ill*, I think. *He used Momma's toothbrush.*

"Now you looking like somebody," the man says, slapping Daddy five. "In fact, you two look just alike," he says, pointing from Daddy to me. "The red hair and the freckles. She yours, all right." He laughs.

I turn my back to that man.

"If you going to take a shower, do it now," Daddy says to his friend. "I made a mess. But there's plenty of hot water left."

I'm watching the man walk to the bathroom. Listening to him and Daddy make jokes, feeling my head tingle and my body get warm all over. I go to tell Mrs. Kim that something ain't right with me, but it's like cotton is stuffed deep down in my throat so the words don't even come out. Next thing I know, I'm lying on the floor and Daddy is patting my face. Saying for Mrs. Kim to call the nurse. Putting his lips close to my ears and saying everything will be okay. Then Momma comes in and tells him to take his mangy hands off me. And by the time I'm back on my feet, Daddy's gone. Like usual.

# CHAPTER SIX

**T**HREE WEEKS HAVE GONE BY since Momma got knocked in the head and I passed out in the hospital. But kids are still talking about it. Teachers that don't hardly know me ask how Momma's doing. Some even took up a collection. They called a television station and told 'em about it too. Cash is still coming in from all over town. Last count, we had almost $5,000.

"Don't act like your momma gonna use all that moola to pay bills," Sato says to me. "We know she headed to Jack's Crazy Cars to get a new ride."

Sato's a tall bowlegged boy who gets smart with me all the time. But I still like him—too much, really.

I tell Sato to mind his own business, even though Momma and me do got the worst-looking ride you ever seen. But inside, I'm smiling big-time. 'Cause we ain't never had this much cash before. And with Momma still out of work, that money's gonna help us pay bills and eat real good for a long time.

It's burning up out here. Eighty-nine degrees, and it's only April. So I roll my can of pop over my forehead to cool off.

Sato asks me how much of the money Momma gave to me. "Maybe she ain't give me nothing," I say, taking a swig of Pepsi.

Sato bust out laughing. "I know your momma ain't that cheap," he says. "Shoot. Even my broke-down mom would give me a few bucks."

I don't tell Sato that Momma gave me six hundred dollars. That she said it was to make up for all the hard times we been through. And for the time she pitched my money out the window like it was trash.

"Give me a taste?" Sato says, reaching for my pop.

I shake my head no. "I don't want your germs."

He takes my arms and wraps 'em around me tight, so it's like I'm hugging my own self. He says he ain't letting go till I give him a sip.

I bend my wrist back as far as I can. Laugh when the pop spills and bubbles out over his arm and onto the ground.

"Oh no you didn't," he says, snatching the can out my hand and running.

I chase that boy two whole blocks before I catch him. By then, half my pop is down his throat.

We both breathing hard, like there ain't enough air out here to go around. "Fifty. Fifty cents," I say, sitting on the steps of a big white church that used to be a movie theater. Trying to make him pay me for the pop.

Sato looks at me with those big, pretty brown eyes of his. I turn away. Stare at a pink daisy growing outta a crack in the side of the step.

For a while, he and me are quiet. We watch people walk up and down the street. Check out a man hosing down his pavement.

"Here," Sato says, pulling change out his pocket.

"Ten cents?! You cheap dog," I say, smacking his arm. Chasing after him again.

I like Sato. I ain't sure he likes me the same way. One minute he's nice, the next minute he's treating me mean. Ja'nae says that's how some boys are. "They don't know how to show what they feel."

When we get to the end of the block, Sato and me sit on the hood of a rusty green convertible with the headlights busted out and all four tires missing.

"Looks like your momma's ride," Sato says, pushing me.

"Least she got one," I say, taking my hair and pushing it out my face. "Your momma's walking, ain't she? Or is that her I see over there thumbing a ride?"

Sato looks across the street, then slaps me five. "You got me," he says, moving closer. When he turns around and looks at the mess in the car we're sitting on, I lean over, close my eyes, and sniff his cologne.

"Somebody's living in here," he says, pointing to the chicken bones, hamburger buns smeared with mustard, and bags of newspaper and cans.

He's right. This here's somebody's house.

"How they stay dry?" he says. "Ain't no windows or roof."

He's looking at me, like I should know just 'cause me and Momma used to be homeless too. "Why you asking me?" I say, as nasty as I can.

"I . . . well . . . sorry," Sato says, playing with the baby hair over his lip.

I never talk about the times when me and Momma lived out on the street. I don't like remembering those days. But I tell Sato that the people who live here probably hang out in the stores during the day, to keep cool. Sleep in the car late at night—not in the homeless shelters or on the street. You can get hurt there.

Sato is looking at me like he feels sorry for me. I stare down at my feet and chew on my lip.

"I saw your dad . . . on the corner downtown," he says, shoving his hands down in his pockets. "He ain't recognize me, though."

I don't want to look at Sato or hear him say something smart about my father, so I start walking. Taking giant steps so he can't keep up. But his legs are twice as long as mine and, ten steps later, he's walking right alongside me. Not talking. Not mouthing off, just walking so close that every once in a while his sweaty arm touches mine. When it do, I get cool all over and chill bumps pop up on my arms.

"My father ain't around all the time neither," he says.

I know about Sato's dad. He lives with them in the summer, when he can get construction work full-time. Come wintertime, he heads for Florida. Works there till it's warm here again.

"It ain't the same," I say. "Your dad is a real dad. My father—he don't care about me."

Sato tries to say it don't matter if I ain't got the kind of father I want, 'cause at least I got Dr. Mitchell and Odd Job. But that ain't the same, I wanna tell him. They ain't *supposed* to take care of me, even though they do sometimes.

When we get to the corner, we stay put for a while. I keep waiting for Sato to say something smart about my dad or me being homeless. He don't. He leans on a car and crosses his legs like he's cool. Then he asks me how many freckles I got.

"I don't know," I say, feeling my face, like I can find out that way.

"Two hundred twenty," he says. And he ain't smiling like he's making it up, neither.

I know my face is red and my right leg is shaking way too much. But that don't keep me from staring right at Sato. Or him from looking at me like I'm the prettiest girl he ever seen.

# CHAPTER SEVEN

THEY HAD A PRETRIAL FOR SHIKETA TODAY—but Momma wasn't there. Just the lawyers and the judge. They wanted to look over Momma's medical records and see what witnesses they might want to call later. Shiketa's lawyer don't want her doing time in jail with grown-up criminals. He wants her to stay in juvey and try to make things right by doing community service. So they're supposed to talk about that too. I hope Shiketa gets ten years for what she done to Momma.

It's been one month and one week since Shiketa hurt Momma, and I think they shoulda had the real trial by now. Momma says to be patient. That she wants to make sure Shiketa gets some help and don't hurt nobody else. But that ain't the whole truth. I know. I seen the letters she wrote to Shiketa. Six of 'em, half-finished and balled up in the trash.

Dear Shiketa, one of 'em said.

> You could have killed me and made it so my
> daughter wouldn't have a mother. Then who
> would take care of her? Nobody. I hope they . . .

All six letters ended just the same. *I hope they* . . . Last night, I filled in the missing words myself. *I hope they put you in jail till you ninety. I hope they make you wash dishes all day long until your fingers shrivel up and fall off like dead leaves. I hope they do to you what you did to Momma.*

I didn't write the words down like Momma. I said them in my mind—not out loud where Momma might hear 'em. She wouldn't like it, even if she might be thinking it herself.

"Hey, Momma," I say, walking up to our apartment building right after school.

Momma's sitting on the top step with a newspaper under her butt, trying to keep her tan pants clean. She's got a tray with a pitcher of lemonade on it, and two tall, skinny glasses with ice cubes almost melted down to nothing.

"Sorry I'm late," I say, digging out the ice and putting a piece in my mouth.

She rubs her neck with her dirty hands. She takes off the new purple scarf she's got on and straightens up the wig she's wearing till her hair grows back in. "That's all right. I—I've been busy."

Momma don't have to tell me what she's been up to. Our pavement is soaking wet. And there's four big bags of dirt and all kinds of flowers sitting out.

"They need to lock Shiketa up for good and throw away the key," I say, spooning sugar onto a piece of lemon and sucking it.

Momma touches the spot Shiketa hit. "Maybe not for good. Just till she learns right from wrong."

My face twists up from the sour lemon. "She knows right from wrong," I say, spitting lemon rind into my hand. "She just don't mind doing wrong."

Momma ain't listening. She's down on the pavement emptying a giant bag of dirt into a big blue flowerpot. "See those plants over there? The yellow snapdragons?" she says, pointing to the tall puffy flowers in a pot close to the house. "The woman across the street liked 'em so much, I took her to the store to get some. We spent half the day digging up her yard and planting 'em."

I'm looking at Momma. Wondering why she ain't learned her lesson the first time with Shiketa. Now here she is getting in folks' business again. Next thing you know that old lady gonna be complaining that the flowers died. Then she gonna come screaming and hollering at us.

Momma comes over to me and gives me a hug. Dirt crumbs roll off her fingers and down the front of my shirt. She tells me she got two new jobs. She lost her other part-time jobs 'cause she couldn't go back to work right after she got hit. She kept saying her head hurt. I think it was something else.

"Where you gonna be working now?" I ask.

"I got a job at the university where I take classes. Six months from now I won't have to pay hardly nothing—anything—to go to school."

Momma's gonna work in the dorms. Buzzing students in and out.

"Crazy hours though," she says, scooping dirt out the bag and putting it in the pot. "Weekends, late nights, daylight."

I bend over and look at Shiketa's place. The girl with the burgundy weave is sitting out front. The other day she told Momma Shiketa might come home on house arrest. I freaked out when I heard that. So

Momma called her lawyer, to see what she could do to make that not happen. So far, so good.

Momma walks up the front steps. "I start working in two weeks. Gonna use the money everyone collected to buy a nice used car."

"Don't use it all," I say, downing my lemonade. "We ain't got that much, you know."

Momma looks at me. Shakes her head. "You have to spend it sometimes, Miss Cheapskate."

When Momma goes in the house to rest awhile, I kick off my sneakers and socks. Then I close my eyes and think about Sato. But that don't last long.

"You got a problem?" I hear someone say.

I know that voice. It's the girl with the burgundy weave. But I keep my eyes shut, even when a handful of dirt smacks me in the chest.

"I asked you a question."

When I open my eyes, Weave Girl is standing right over me with her fist pulled back. "My sister Shiketa coulda been home by now if it wasn't for your mother."

I scoot back on my hands and feet. She walks down the steps and rips Momma's flowers out the pot. Ten daffodils come flying my way.

"My mother planted those!"

Weave Girl comes up to me and pokes her finger in my cheek. Her long nail feels like it's a knife. "Your mother need to mind her own business."

Weave Girl ain't as old as Shiketa. She's, like, fifteen. Them two call each other sister, even though they ain't. She's hardcore, with big muscles in her arms and legs like maybe she runs track or plays baseball. But I don't care. I'm tired of people treating me and Momma any way they want. "Leave me alone," I shout.

She pushes me. I get up and give her what she gave me. Then I swallow hard and get ready to get my butt kicked.

Both her fists go up. "You think you bad, huh?" she says, moving 'em back and forth like she's trying to figure out where to hit me first.

"Raspberry?" Momma says, sticking her head out the window. "Get in here!"

Weave Girl steps back.

"And you. What's your name?" Momma asks, coming to the front door.

"Miracle," she says. "Shiketa's sister."

Momma bends down and starts picking up flowers. She tells Miracle that she owes her three dollars.

Miracle smacks her lips like Momma can forget ever seeing *that* money.

Momma puts her arms around me and tells Miracle that she better leave now.

Miracle takes her foot and smashes the daffodils like bugs. "Or what? You gonna call the police on me?"

Sweat sneaks out from under Momma's wig and rolls down her neck. "Please leave," she says. "Right now!"

"Shiketa *better* not do no time." Miracle smiles, fingers her weave, and walks down the steps.

I tell Momma she needs to call up the judge and tell him to give Shiketa life. She says we can't make Shiketa pay for what Miracle's just done.

"Why? Miracle's gonna make me and you pay for what the judge does to Shiketa. And she ain't gonna care nothing 'bout what's fair, and what's not."

# CHAPTER EIGHT

MING AND JA'NAE MOVING SO SLOW toward the bus after
school that when we get on to go home, we gotta
stand up. People on this thing are packed as close as
clothes in a closet—so it's kind of funky, you know.
Ja'nae wants the driver to cut on the air. He won't.
It's only the middle of May. "Too soon," he says, even
though it's eighty-three degrees out and smelly pits
are stinking up the place.

When a seat near us is finally empty, Sato sits his
skinny butt in it. Ming ain't like that. When the boy
in front of him gets up, Ming moves aside to let Ja'nae
sit down. I tell Sato that he shoulda done the same
thing for me. He says, "Ja'nae and Ming go together.
Me and you ain't got it going on like that."

Ming is Mai's brother. Him and Ja'nae been

boyfriend and girlfriend for two years now. He works on his parents' food truck, right by the school. But he rides the bus eight stops outta his way, just to be with Ja'nae, then walks back to work. Sato tells Ming that he's the dumbest boy he ever met. Ming says, "That's aaight, but I got me a girl, now don't I?"

You'd think Sato would be embarrassed letting me stand here with this heavy book bag while he sitting down. But he ain't. He talking his head off. Asking about Momma. Telling me to tell her that he gonna come by our place to visit her soon. I'm hoping it's me he really wants to see.

Ja'nae waves her finger for me to lean down so she can tell me something. "Don't pay Sato no attention. He likes you. A lot."

My eyes go from Sato's new black sneakers, to his purple tee, to his smooth, brown lips.

Ja'nae pulls her long braids off her neck. "Some boys act tough 'cause they don't want girls knowing how much they really like 'em."

A woman gets up. I sit down. Sato scoots over next to me. Puts his lips too close to my ear when he asks what me and Ja'nae are talking about. He can't whisper, though, so of course Ja'nae hears him.

"We talking 'bout the class trip," she lies.

Sato thinks they might cancel it. "Not enough people signed up."

He don't know what he's talking about. In three weeks, we'll be in Canada with no parents.

Sato asks us who we rooming with, since he's rooming with Ming. Mai is rooming with Ja'nae. I'm supposed to room with Zora, I tell him.

Ja'nae puts her arm around my shoulder. Her hot breath tickles my ear when she says that Zora don't wanna room with me now. "If I even say your name, she acts like she wants to hit me."

Sato is minding our business. "Zora mad at *you*?"

"Yep," Ja'nae says, pulling out a cotton ball and wiping vanilla perfume on her neck and arms. "She—"

"She what?" I say, trying to see what Ja'nae knows.

Ja'nae drops the cotton on the floor and kicks it under the seat. "She won't say what you did. Just that you better not say nothing to her."

Zora hasn't mentioned the money to me yet, but she don't treat me the same no more. At lunchtime, she sits at another table. When we all walk to class, she makes sure she don't end up walking next to me. I asked her the other day what her problem was, wondering if she was really gonna tell me. She just said, "You know," and walked away from me.

Ja'nae takes Ming's hand in hers. "It was something bad, wasn't it?"

I change the subject, 'cause I ain't gonna tell Ja'nae what I done, and I ain't gonna give Zora the money back neither. Anyhow, it's about time she got some of the bad luck that's been following me around.

"Who wanna buy some pretzels?" I ask, pulling pretzels out my bag. Greedy Sato wants some, but don't want to pay. Next thing I know he's talking to Ming about going to the food truck for free food.

Ming tells Sato he will hook him up with *dak bulgogi* and *bean deh toe*.

Sato frowns. "What?"

"Barbecued chicken and fried onion pancakes," Ming says, rubbing his stomach.

Sato asks if Mai will be there.

When Ming laughs, his eyes disappear just like Mai's. "Yep. My mom's keeping an eye on her. Says she's getting too sneaky."

"Forget it, then," Sato says, shaking his head. "She's too evil."

Ja'nae gets on Sato's case. Says he'd be evil too if some girl cut his hair off, stuffed it in plastic bags, and taped them to the girls'-room mirror, the way they did to Mai at the beginning of the school year.

Ming gets up, pulls down on the cord till the driver tells him to knock it off. "I went after that girl's brother, didn't I?" Ming says. "And Mai got mad about that, too."

Ja'nae is right behind Ming, telling him that Mai didn't wanna make things worse by dragging other people into her business. Then the two of 'em get off the bus.

Sato asks me what the note taped next to Mai's hair said. I ain't never gonna forget it, mean as it was. "Hard times at Mai (My) House. Human hair for sale. One bag for a dolla. Three bags for two-fiddy."

Sato gets on me. He says we all Mai's friends, so we shoulda went after them girls and whipped their butts good.

He's right. But none of us can fight, and them girls were bigger than us—eleventh graders. Anyhow, Mai said to leave it alone. She didn't want no more trouble. But she ain't been the same since. She been suspended three times and things between her father and her are worse than ever. We keep telling her to chill. Not to get so upset over what people say about her being mixed and all. She says we don't know how it feels, always having people look and point—asking about your skin color and hair before they even ask your name.

"I don't care what people say about me," Sato says, standing up to leave. "I know I look good."

When the door opens, I push him off the bus. Tell him he needs to look in the mirror sometime. But I don't let on what I'm really thinking. That I like him so much it hurts.

# CHAPTER NINE

**SATO AND I DON'T GO STRAIGHT HOME.** We head for Odd Job's place. The barbecue wings cooking on the grill make Sato smack his lips. He wants me to get Odd Job to hook him up with some water ice and chicken. I look at him like he crazy. "Yeah. Just like you did me that favor on the bus and gave me your seat," I say.

"Aaaa, girl," Sato says, showing off them pretty white teeth. "I was just trying to treat you like we equals. Not baby you, like you was a girl or something."

Odd Job ain't got no regular store. He got his whole operation set up on this street corner lot. He ain't selling frozen Kool-Aid out a cooler like he did last spring. Now he got a water-ice stand with a big orange umbrella attached to it. And besides washing cars, he got his boys working the grill—a big, rusty trash can he split in half and put high up on sticks.

"Please?" Sato says, getting up in my face. Making it so I can't think straight. "I would do it for *you*," he says, still trying to get me to hook him up with food.

Odd Job's scraping and scooping up balls of lime-green water ice and putting 'em into cups. "Raspberry Girl. How's Momma? I called her a few times. Woulda come visit her in the hospital too, but I don't do stuff like that," he says, handing the water ice to me and Sato.

"I don't like green all that much," Sato says, eating it anyway.

Odd Job wipes sweat from his forehead with a ripped-up shirt he pulls out his back pocket. "It's free, ain't it?" He turns my way. "Hospitals ain't my thing. I break into a cold sweat every time I go inside one," he says. "Couldn't even go in when my mother was dying. My brothers and sisters still mad at me for that."

Sato goes and sits down in Odd Job's lounge chair. Pulls back the stick and crosses his legs like he's sitting in his own living room.

"Get your crusty butt out my chair," Odd Job yells.

Sato stays put. Odd Job don't tell him again to get

moving. He asks me some more about Momma. Says he told her not to worry 'bout the rent.

Odd Job, Dr. Mitchell, and Momma grew up in the projects together. He looks out for us. When we had to leave the PJ's and couldn't get that Section Eight house we wanted, he let us move into one of his apartment buildings. He don't charge us hardly nothing. He says Momma can make up the difference by cleaning up the two vacant units in the building. They nasty, though, and Momma ain't had the nerve to go at 'em yet.

"Momma's doing okay."

"Your daddy been by?"

I get mad when he asks that. "He don't know where we live!"

Odd Job tells me to chill. Not to get all excited. "If he show up, y'all call me. I'll take care of things."

I don't ask what that means. I just nod my head yes. Then he pulls out twenty-five dollars and says for me to give it to Momma.

"Sure," I say, smelling the money before I stuff it in my pocket.

Sato walks over to us with lime-green lips and teeth. "Can you hook a brother up with another water ice?"

Odd Job looks at him like he lost his mind. But he don't say nothing, 'cause three cars pull up at once. Five little girls get outta the first car. The oldest one only looks six years old. Two of 'em start whining to their dad about wanting some chicken.

"A little help here, please," Odd Job says, looking our way.

I ask the girls what they want. They all start talking at once. I tell 'em to shut up. Sato says that he can tell I ain't used to being around little kids. He has five brothers and two sisters. He's the oldest.

Sato leans down and picks up the smallest one. She's maybe three years old. "You want something to drink, too?" he says, tickling her belly.

She wraps her arms around his neck. Whispers something in his ear. Then starts playing with his earring.

I wait on the second car and Odd Job takes care of the people who come out the third one. Everybody wants their stuff *now*. Nobody's got exact change. A few of the grown-ups are complaining about the prices and trying to swing a deal with Odd Job. They wasting their breath. Odd Job don't change his prices for nobody, 'cept maybe me and Momma.

Before we know anything, everybody is gone.

Odd Job turns to Sato and asks what flavor water ice he wants. He gives him a giant-sized cup piled high with the rainbow-colored kind. I have to ask him for a refill.

He's got his arm around Sato's neck, telling him that he likes how he handles kids. Next thing I know he's asking him if he wants a summer job.

Sato looks all happy. He says his mother told him he better find hisself a job. Odd Job gets his boys to bring over two sizzling hot chicken sandwiches. He hands me one and asks why I'm so quiet. I'm just thinking, that's all, how nice it's gonna be working with Sato all summer.

Odd Job's pinching my nose. "Raspberry Swirl, what you grinning at, girl?"

"Nothing," I say, licking my lips. Glad they ain't too dry or ashy.

"Nothing," Sato says, repeating after me, then winking, like he's thinking the same thing.

# CHAPTER TEN

MOMMA'S SITTING IN THE KITCHEN with her wig hanging from her hand and her head down on the table. She don't answer when I ask how she's doing. I drop my backpack. Run over and ask what's wrong. She lifts her head up and says she's fine—just got another headache, is all. But her eyes are red. Puffy, too.

Fat, juicy sausages lie in a plate on top of the stove. Thick, white, sticky water oozes from under a boiling pot of covered rice. My words come out fast. "You sick? Need some aspirin?"

"Clean your room," Momma says. "Zora and her dad will be here soon."

My tongue feels as thick as the sausages. "You sure *you* okay?" I ask in a voice as soft as the butter melting beside the stove.

Momma takes the top off the rice and sprinkles a pinch of sugar in it. "He found us."

Rice water bubbles up and runs over the sides of the pot. The fire jumps and sizzles.

I know who *he* is. Momma don't even have to say his name.

"I opened the door, and there he was."

I push my fingernails deep into my arm. "How come he just can't leave us alone?"

Momma cuts the fire off. Comes over and holds me close. "Your father used to be somebody," she says, clearing her throat. "When he walked down the street with that red hair and pretty smile, people stared. Wondered who that good-looking man was."

I push her away. Run to my room and get my stash from underneath the faded blue linoleum rug. Quarters drop on the kitchen floor when I run back in there asking Momma if Daddy tried to get money off her.

She bends down and picks up the change. "Yeah, money. Always money."

I follow her into the dining room, sit down at the table, and spread my money out. Momma didn't give him a dime. That's what she tells me. She packed him seven sandwiches and a jar of Kool-Aid. Handed him some soap and a washcloth and told him he could wash up with the hose in the backyard.

"He's just like Shiketa," I say. "He ain't gonna let us live in peace."

Momma reaches for my face. "You look just like him."

I turn away. Ask her not to say stuff like that.

"Don't you remember the silly songs he made up? Him riding you on his back up and down the street?"

I cover my ears to keep her words out my head. But I'm thinking 'bout stuff, too. Like the time he picked me up early from school, and took me to the zoo to feed the bears, and eat blueberry cotton candy and taffy apples. I gave him sticky kisses. He ain't wash 'em off all day long.

I pick up two pennies I dropped. "I'm not like him, am I?"

Momma's eyes move all over my face. "No, not all that much," she says, walking into the living room. She picks up magazines and stacks 'em in a neat pile on the glass coffee table she hauled in from somebody else's trash. I lay on the couch, turn over on my stomach, and reach for a piece of purple stationery lying on the floor.

Dear Shiketa,

When I was your age, I went to school. I worked
two jobs. I didn't beat people up. My head hurts a
lot now. And I'm trying not to hate you, but . . .

I drop the letter when Momma sits down on the
couch. I ask her why she's writing Shiketa all the time.

"It's private." That's all she says, like I ain't got
the right to know. Then she takes the letter and walks
out the room.

I kick pillows off the couch. Knock the magazines
back on the floor. "You *should* hate her, for what she
done."

When she comes back, she hands me a glass of
apple juice. Steps over the magazines, sits down, and
tells me that it helped her seeing Daddy today. "Made
me see how good we got it, you and me."

I look around the place. Check out the chipped
yellow paint around the windows and the brown spot
on the ceiling from where the roof leaked before we
moved in.

"It ain't much," she says, smiling, "but it's clean
and it's ours, for now anyhow. And we not, *we're* not
gonna let anybody—not your daddy or Shiketa—
chase us off. Not no more."

Tears roll down my cheeks. "They never gonna leave us alone. And I get so mad about it that sometimes I could just . . ."

Momma's finger is up to her lips. "Shhh. Sniff."

I wipe the tears away. "What? Something stink?"

"Close your eyes and smell."

I shut my eyes and breathe in. Something sweet and pretty fills my nose.

"Flowers. Our flowers," she says, closing my eyes when I open 'em. Leaning my head on her shoulder like I'm a baby. "We can make something sweet and good out of all the mess around us. If we want."

I sniff again. Ask Momma if that's the lilac bush I smell or the roses we planted out back the other day. Momma says she ain't sure. That we can go out back and see. But neither one of us moves. We sit for another half hour, holding each other.

I got my eyes closed, but my mind won't keep still. I'm trying to figure out how come Momma's writing letters to Shiketa, and what my father's really up to. I don't say none of this to Momma. I can see from the letters, she's more upset than she's letting on. Maybe scared too, of what she might do if she don't act like everything is just fine and dandy.

# CHAPTER ELEVEN

Dr. Mitchell said Zora didn't want to come to dinner. She had a headache and stayed at home with the housekeeper. "I think she just said that," he says, kissing Momma when he comes in the house. "But I didn't argue."

Momma's wig is back on her head, and her eyes are clear since she put drops in 'em. "Is Zora mad at us or something?" she asks Dr. Mitchell. "The last two times you came over she wasn't with you."

Dr. Mitchell looks at me. "You two fighting?"

"Not me," I say, washing my hands at the kitchen sink.

Momma is over by the fridge with Dr. Mitchell, handing him lettuce and cucumbers to wash. Telling me to call Zora and at least say hi. I give her this fake smile. Say I'll do it later.

"Now," she says, handing me the dish towel. "Dinner's still gonna be a while."

Dr. Mitchell wants us to straighten things out. "Your mother and I aren't going to stop seeing each other just because you two aren't getting along."

I tell them that maybe Zora's scared to come over because of what happened the last time she was here. Her dad says that ain't it. "It's something between you and her. I know it. But she's not saying. You neither, I see."

They looking at me like I'm lying. Momma hands me the phone and says, "Call her."

I wanna tell 'em you can't make people be friends. They gotta want to. When I dial the phone and start walking to my bedroom, my hands begin to shake.

"Talk to her out here," Momma says.

Dr. Mitchell rips the lettuce in two and tells Momma to stop being so nosy. "Let them work it out."

"Zora?" I say, when she picks up the phone.

"What do you want?"

I want to hang up the phone. I don't. "Your dad said for me to call."

"What?"

I go outside and sit on the front steps, till I see Momma by the window trying to listen in. Then I come back inside and go to my room.

"They want us to make up."

Zora's quiet for a while. "Who?"

She knows who I'm talking about. She's just trying to be smart. I tell her that too. She hangs up the phone. I call her *right* back.

"You stole my money," she says, not even asking who's on the phone first.

I lie. Tell her that it wasn't me. "Maybe you lost it or something."

I'm waiting for her to hang up again. Or call me a liar. She asks to talk to her dad. I go to my bedroom door, look at Dr. Mitchell in front of the TV watching baseball and cutting up tomatoes.

"Why?" I ask.

"Just put him on."

I know I should give Zora back her money. But I'm not gonna. Anyhow, she don't need it. She got everything. Too much, really. All I got is Momma. So I lay the phone on the bed and don't pick it up for fifteen minutes. Zora's gone by then.

When I hang the phone up in the kitchen Momma

asks how things are between me and Zora. "You two friends again?"

"Yeah," I say, heading outside to be with Dr. Mitchell. His car alarm went off and he went to check on things.

Dr. Mitchell's on the steps looking at Miracle and some boys sitting in front of their place. He thinks they messed with his ride and made the alarm go off. He says he don't want no trouble outta them every time he comes to visit. "Otherwise I might have to use my bat again." He laughs.

He just came from the barbershop, so you can smell the lotion on his head. It's sweeter than Momma's flowers.

Momma's at the window. She wants us to come inside and wash up before we eat. We stay put. Dr. Mitchell's telling me about the time he lived in the PJ's and got chased home by some boys who wanted his new sneakers. He's moving his arms and legs like he's running. "I only had those sneakers eight hours before they stole 'em right off my feet."

Momma keeps bugging us. Saying the food's gonna get cold. Dr. Mitchell stands up to go inside, then backtracks and goes down the steps. He wipes dried mud off Momma's new Escort. It's got

100,000 miles on it, but it's better than what we had.

"You coming?" he asks, walking back up the steps. I'm right behind him. Thinking he smells just like my father did after he came from the barbershop on Saturdays. I reach for his hand. He holds tight to mine, and I pretend he's my real dad, and he ain't *never* gonna leave me.

We go to the kitchen to wash our hands, all three of us. Dr. Mitchell leans over and kisses Momma right where Shiketa hit her. "You look good to me," he says, giving her a pinch.

"Eat up," Momma says, passing the rice. I take two big spoonsful, then hand the bowl to Dr. Mitchell, and I don't feel bad one little bit that Zora ain't here with us.

# CHAPTER TWELVE

**S**HIKETA AIN'T GOING TO JAIL. The judge gave her six months in juvey and a year of community service. Shiketa got a bad attitude, so he wants her put away to teach her a lesson.

"Be glad you're not headed to jail, young lady," the judge says. "When you hit this woman in the head, you committed assault and battery."

"That ain't fair!" I say so loud even the judge hears me. "She should go to a real jail."

The judge says for me to quiet down or get out.

Momma asks to speak. The judge is real nice to her. Tells her to take her time.

Shiketa's whole family is here—dressed in suits and fancy dresses like they going to church. Miracle is over there too. Rolling her eyes at me every chance she gets.

"Well, Your Honor," Momma says, rubbing her hands and squeezing her fingers while she talks. "Shiketa ain't a bad girl. I mean, she isn't a bad girl. She just doesn't have any guidance."

A woman in a peach pants suit jumps up and says that ain't so. "Shiketa got plenty folks looking out for her. But she hardheaded. Wants to do what she wants to do."

The judge hits the gavel on the desk. "Quiet."

Momma clears her throat. Touches the spot where Shiketa hit her on the head. "Shiketa's not bad, Your Honor. But how'd a seventeen-year-old get to live all by herself? Where's she getting the money? Nobody's answered that question yet."

The judge looks over at Shiketa's lawyer. He stands up and says Shiketa wouldn't obey her mother's rules, so she put her out. "Shiketa worked two jobs, Your Honor. At McDonald's and a Laundromat near her apartment."

The judge looks over at Shiketa's mother. Asks her if she can handle Shiketa when she's released from juvey.

"She can stay as long as she don't act up like before," her mother says, crossing her legs. "If she disobeys my rules, she gone."

Momma keeps talking, saying Shiketa needs to go someplace else once she gets out of juvey. "Where she can learn to read better and get her G.E.D."

"I can read," Shiketa snaps. "So mind your own business."

The judge slams the gavel down again. "You," he says, pointing to Shiketa. "You do your six months and community service, and then I want you back here for placement in a group home." He points to Shiketa's social worker. "Have something in place. Don't come back here with your hands empty."

Momma sits down next to me. She holds my hand and says, "Maybe she's gonna have a chance now."

I don't know. I think Momma just made things worse. Shiketa's looking back at us and saying something we can't hear. Miracle's shaking her head, like she can't believe what just happened.

When we get outside, Momma asks me if I wanna go for ice cream. I just wanna get away from here. Shiketa's people are right behind us. I don't want them starting nothing.

"Hey, you. Wait up." It's Shiketa's mother. She

got on shoes so tall and pointy, it looks like she could stab you with the heel or the toe. "What's your name again?" she says, lighting up a cigarette right in Momma's face.

"Mrs. Hill," Momma says, fanning smoke away.

"Well, Miz Hill, my daughter was raised just right. I sent her to school with all my other kids. They graduated. Working now too. But Shiketa got a hard head. So naturally, hard times gonna follow somebody like that."

Momma is not as tall as this woman. And even though Momma's dressed real nice, her clothes look like rags next to hers.

"I wasn't trying to say you didn't raise Shiketa right."

"Yes, you did," one of Shiketa's sisters says. "I heard you say it right in there. And you wrong too," she says, playing with three little gold bracelets she's wearing.

Momma starts to walk away. Then stops. She tells Shiketa's mother that Shiketa's only a child and she don't need to have her own place and be paying her own way. She needs somebody to look after her. "To make sure she goes to school and does the right thing."

The woman moves closer to Momma. "People like you get on my last nerve," she says. "Thinking you can do better. Acting like you better too."

I tell Momma to come on and let's go. But before we do, Miracle walks over and gives us her two cents. "She like to play rich," she says, pointing to Momma. "Planting all them flowers. Sweeping up all the time and minding other folks' business."

Shiketa's mother steps in front of Miracle and tells her to go someplace else. "You think you can do better by Shiketa?" she says, holding a finger in Momma's face. The one with the big diamond ring on it. "Take her. Let her come live with you once she does her time. Then we'll see how much you know 'bout raising kids."

I don't move. Not even to look Momma's way. 'Cause I'm so scared she gonna say, "Okay, when Shiketa gets out she can come live with us."

"Well," Momma says, taking her time talking. "If I had the room . . ."

Shiketa's mom throws down her lit cigarette and stomps it. "See? Y'all kind always talking. But never do step up to the plate when the time comes."

Momma turns around and heads down the steps. Stops. Walks back up to Shiketa's mom and says,

"She's your child. Raise her, like I raised mine. And don't be expecting me to do your job."

Miracle's mouth is hanging open. Shiketa's sisters look like they wanna smack me and Momma. Her mother stands there saying that Momma ain't nothing but talk.

We take off down the steps.

"They following us?" Momma says, pulling me by the hand.

I look back. "No. They still standing there."

"Good," she says, walking faster. "Let's hurry up, 'fore they do."

# CHAPTER THIRTEEN

Mᴏᴍᴍᴀ ᴀɴᴅ ᴍᴇ ᴡᴇɴᴛ ᴏᴜᴛ ᴛᴏ ᴇᴀᴛ, so it was late when we got home from the trial. Miracle was sitting on our front steps by then. We had to ask her to give us room so we could get into our *own* place. I was mad. Momma, too. But she ain't wanna start no trouble. So we went inside and stayed there.

By the time it was dark, our steps were almost full. Miracle and her friends was there acting up, celebrating 'cause Shiketa got off light, not having to go to county jail. The noise was so bad we couldn't hear the TV unless we turned it up full blast.

"I'm calling the cops," Momma says.

I beg her not to. "You do that, and somebody gonna hurt you again. Maybe worse this time."

One o'clock in the morning we smell weed.

Miracle's still out front mouthing off. Drinking wine straight out a bottle and saying they should take all Momma's stupid flowers and throw 'em into the street. "Then bust up that junk car she bought."

Momma can't sleep. Me neither. So one minute she's in the kitchen looking for something good to eat. The next minute she's cleaning. She's already done all the woodwork and cleaned out the stove. I tell her we need to just go to bed. But that won't make no sense, 'cause we not gonna be able to sleep nohow.

Come two o'clock in the morning, I tell Momma she should call Dr. Mitchell or Odd Job.

"No. You want them hurt? These kids just looking for trouble tonight. Anybody that comes by here's gonna find it too."

I sit by the window and peek out under the curtain. Miracle's sitting on our car. Some boy is holding her around the waist, kissing her hard. Her girlfriend asks her if she got a light. A cigarette lighter flies from her hands over to the steps.

"We should burn the whole place down. The whole street," Miracle says, pushing the boy away. Walking up our steps and sitting down.

Momma tells me to get away from the window.

"Shiketa's my girl. We like this," Miracle says,

crossing her fingers. "That witch," she says, pointing to our house, "act like she owns the neighborhood and everybody gotta do things her way."

The wine's getting to Miracle, I guess. 'Cause all of a sudden she starts to cry. "Shiketa and me like sisters. She don't make me pay rent. Just cook and clean. Now I'm gonna get kicked out unless money start coming in."

Miracle's girls tell her to stop acting like a punk. Then somebody reminds her that landlords can't throw you out even when you don't pay up. "Not for six or eight months, at least."

Momma sits down on the floor by me and looks out the window too. We hold our breath when Miracle walks up to the door and kicks it. "Y'all come out here! Now!"

Momma's eyes get big.

It's Miracle's fist on the door now. *Bam. Bam. Bam.*

"I'm calling the police," Momma says, heading for the kitchen on her hands and knees.

I'm right behind her. Crawling like a baby. Telling her the police will come but Miracle won't go nowhere. "She still gonna be living up the street tomorrow."

We go back to the window. Peek out under the blinds.

"Y'all crazy over there, making all that noise." It's Miz Evelyn, Momma's friend from across the street. She got a phone in her hand. "I'm calling the police. Don't think I'm playing."

Miracle backs off. "We just having a little fun. Dag." She sits down on the top steps again.

"Why don't you go to your own building? Leave that nice woman alone."

One of Miracle's friends cusses. Tells Miracle she's bored anyhow and they need to get going. Miz Evelyn slams the door shut. Me and Momma don't move.

It's three o'clock in the morning and Momma's still sitting at the window. She's asleep. Her arms are holding her legs and her head's leaning against the windowsill. Every once in a while, I gotta push her up straight, so she don't fall over.

Now Miracle's friends are joking 'round with her about being homeless. "You gonna be living in a shelter? Well, don't worry, Boo. We'll come over and visit you," one of them kids says.

I can't see Miracle living in a shelter or on the streets. She too cute for that.

"I'm going to bed," Momma says.

I stay at the window till Miracle's gone, an hour later. Then I go to Momma's room to cut off the light. She's asleep. There's a pen in her hand and balled-up stationery all over the floor.

~~Dear Shiketa:~~

~~I don't like you. I don't like your friend Miracle. I try to live a decent life and all you do is make things dirty and loud. I'm tired of the both of you.~~

Dear Shiketa,

Your friends scared us tonight—but we're still here. Nobody can make us leave before we're ready.

You are smart—I know, we used to talk a lot. But you need different friends if you want a different kind of life once you get out. Remember— you deserve better.

I want to wake Momma up and tell her to cross off the sweet stuff she wrote and rewrite the part that says she don't like Shiketa or Miracle. I want her to not be nice to them. To take a stick and hit them good. To make Shiketa's mom cry at night, like I do sometimes thinking about what happened, and what could've happened to me if Momma had died or something.

Momma wakes up. Rubs her eyes and asks what I'm doing in her room. I'm holding the letter behind my back. Telling her I just came to kiss her good night.

"I love you," she says, pulling me into bed with her.

"Love you too," I say. I drop the letter to the floor. Momma's so close and warm.

"Raspberry," she says, yawning.

"Yeah, Momma?"

"One day, things will settle down for us. All this craziness will be over. You wait and see."

I tickle her. She tickles me back. "I know, Momma," I say, laughing, not hardly paying no mind to the sirens screaming as a fire truck races up our street.

# CHAPTER FOURTEEN

Since the trial and Miracle's party, Momma's changed her mind about a few things. First off, she wanna move. Now. Not just 'cause Daddy knows where we live, or 'cause she's tired of dealing with Shiketa and Miracle. "Just 'cause I want you safe and not filled with worry all the time," she says.

So Momma talked to the lawyer again. Told her she wants us in that Section Eight house in Pecan Landings before school starts up in September. It's June 3rd now.

I don't know what's gonna happen with the new house or Miracle or my father neither. All I know is, can't nobody take care of me and Momma, but me and Momma. So when Momma leaves the house to go to her job pressing clothes at the dry cleaners, I hit the streets. Knock on every door on our block. All twenty-five of 'em.

People 'round here sleep late on Saturdays. So some folks never do answer the door when I show up wanting to know if they'll pay me to sweep or hose down their sidewalks. Other folks just hang their heads out the window and call me every name they can think of. But six people, mostly old dried-up women, say for me to go ahead. I make me thirty dollars in two hours. Not as much as I want, so instead of going to Mai's house and heading for the mall like I planned, I knock on one more door. I ask the man who answers if he wants his pavement done.

"What?" he says, coughing and hacking. Spitting yellow snot onto the pavement.

"My name is Raspberry Hill," I say, repeating myself again. "I live up the block. For ten dollars, I'll clean your walk. Wash it down. Scrub it clean. You know."

This man ain't old like the women. He's like, thirty. Got a black do-rag tied 'round his head and big gold hoop earrings on. "I oughta . . ." he says, making a face so mean I take a step back. "Girl, I just got to bed. And you out here hustling . . . waking me up for some stupid stuff. If you don't get . . ."

I'm down his crooked steps and two houses over before he slams the door shut. "Forget you!" I yell, crossing the street and knocking on Miz Evelyn's door.

"Your momma want something?" she says, holding her hand over her eyes to block the sun.

I shake my head no. Say I was just wondering if she needed any help doing stuff around her place.

"Ain't you nice," she says, grabbing my cheek and pinching it. "Just like your mother."

When Miz Evelyn walks, one leg goes high up in the air, then down again like she trying not to step on poop or something. She's pretty, for somebody her age. Got long silver-blue hair past her shoulders. Big, fat teeth—fake ones, probably. Her skin is the color of pecan shells.

"I was thinking just the other day," she says, taking me 'round back to the yard, "somebody needs to clean this here alley."

She holds her nose and unlocks a gray wooden fence with faded red apples painted all over it. Garbage is everywhere—like somebody threw trash bags out the windows, just to see how far the food would fly when the bags smashed to the ground like water balloons.

"It's a shame, ain't it?" Miz Evelyn says, taking my hand. "The junkies be back here sometimes, you know, sleeping in all this filth."

I think about Daddy. Wonder if he hanging out in places like this.

"Your mother send you?" she asks, bending down and picking up a rusty corn can. "'Cause she said she would, you know."

I stop following her, 'cause it's too nasty out here. "No," I say, checking the bottom of my sneakers.

"Poor thing. Musta forgot. Said she was gonna send you by a few weeks ago. To help me spray flowers. Bugs like the roses, you know."

I tell Miz Evelyn I was just out trying to make some money. Wanted to know if she needed help with something. But I can't clean up the alley. "You need a bunch of people to do that."

She uses her skirt for a trash bag. Holds up the bottom and drops old cans and pieces of paper in it. "I do what I can."

I let her know that I can't stay long. 'Cause I got stuff to do. She keeps walking up the alley, saying she's seen the alley behind our house. How clean it is. That's 'cause Momma been doing it since we moved here last year. Even made Dr. Mitchell and Odd Job come help one weekend. "It's easier to keep it clean, once you get it good and clean," she says.

"Well, I gotta go," I say, telling her she needs to go inside too 'cause it ain't safe back here.

Miz Evelyn doesn't follow me. She says for me to let myself out. And to take a few quarters out the candy dish in the hallway, "'cause your family's been so nice to me." She got a whole bunch of quarters, too. So many that they running over the sides of the dish and piling up on the table and floor. I stand there awhile, counting 'em in my head. I stop at twenty-five bucks, but there's way more than that. I pick up about twenty dollars' worth and walk out the door, jingling the change in my pocket like I ain't got a care in the world.

# CHAPTER FIFTEEN

**S**ATO CALLED. IT'S THE FIRST TIME that boy ever picked up the phone and dialed my number. I am so happy. Momma's working out back in the garden. We haven't seen Miracle for two whole weeks and things are going pretty good. So him calling makes this week extra special.

"I was thinking 'bout you," he says. "And I didn't have nothing else to do, so I called."

"Good."

Sato says he's on his front porch watching two little girls jumping double Dutch.

I walk outside. Look up and down the street for Miracle. She ain't there.

"You get your money back from the class trip?" he asks.

"Yeah," I say.

Not enough people signed up for the trip, so they canceled it. I gave Dr. Mitchell's money to Zora, so she would know I'm not a thief.

Sato covers the phone and talks to somebody else for a minute. "I wasn't going nohow. Here."

He hands the phone to somebody. It's a boy. A little one. His brother, I guess. He is so small, all he says in the phone is "Hi. Hi."

"That's my baby brother. He's three. A twin."

I walk over to the snapdragons and pull three out the dirt. Hold 'em under my nose and smile at how sweet they are. Sato asks about Momma. How she's doing. I tell him about the letters.

"I wouldn't write to somebody that smashed me in the head," he says.

I walk down the steps and over to the back fence. Momma's carrying a big plant with its roots hanging out like thin, white veins. "I don't think she mails 'em."

Sato says that's worse. "To write letters you know you ain't sending. So what she writing 'em for?"

I go back to my seat and look at Miz Evelyn waving at me. I turn around and go inside. "They shoulda let us go on the class trip. I wanted to go someplace different. Not be around here all the time."

It turns out that Sato didn't have enough money to go. He says he was gonna have a party all by hisself when we took off for Canada. "I already started stashing things. Chips. Cookies. Pop."

I ask Sato how it feels to have other people in the house besides grown-ups. To not be the only child. He says it ain't bad. But he's the oldest, so it feels like he's the only one sometimes. "My ten-year-old brother shares a room with me. He's too young for me to talk to about guy stuff. But if my mom gets on my nerves, or my dad is gone too long, me and him talk about that."

Usually I talk to my girls about everything, but since I took Zora's money, I don't feel right calling Ja'nae and Mai up. Or telling 'em that I'm scared something else bad is gonna happen to Momma and me. They might ask me about the money. And I don't want to talk about that.

"When I'm grown, I'm gonna have two kids. A boy and a girl," Sato says.

"I'm having six."

"And I'm gonna live in a big house, with four bathrooms, eight fireplaces, and a refrigerator so big it'll have four doors on it."

I go to my bedroom, lay across my bed, and put my feet up on the wall. "My house is gonna be all by itself. Not attached to the next house, like this one. And it's gonna be in the woods."

"In the woods? Don't ask me to visit you."

"Well. Maybe not in the woods. But surrounded by trees. Bad things don't happen to people in houses with lots of trees nearby."

Sato says I'm nuts. "In the movies, it's the houses in the woods where people end up cut to pieces and—"

"Oh, yeah. I forgot. Then I want to live in the city, in a house not connected to another house. I want lots of flowers and lots of children . . ."

"And a husband, right?"

"Right. And Momma, too. She's gotta be there."

Sato's back to talking 'bout his house. How his wife ain't gonna work, like his mother. "She's gonna stay home."

"What if she don't want to? What if she wants to be a lawyer, like Zora's mom? Or have two jobs, like my mother?"

"Your mother likes working all them jobs?"

I have to think a minute. "No. But if she had one

good job, not two that don't pay all that well, she would like it, I bet."

Sato's mind is made up. His wife's gonna stay home and take care of the kids. "Not work and cook and clean and care for a million kids, like my mom."

I tell Sato that I'm gonna do both. "Work, take time off and have kids. Then go back to work when they're ten."

Sato says he could be down with something like that. But he ain't sure. I lay on my stomach and quarters fall out my pocket. For a minute, I want to tell Sato everything about the money I stole off Zora and Miz Evelyn. How sometimes I really do wish my father was here living with us. Taking care of us.

Momma calls me. She needs help in the garden. "I gotta go."

"Me too, Raspberry Curl."

I bite down on my lip. "You gonna call me back sometime?"

Sato's quiet. "Sometime," he says, laughing. "Sometime I just might call you again, Raspberry Swirl."

I don't hang up when he does. 'Cause I can still hear him, saying my name.

# CHAPTER SIXTEEN

**WE ONLY GOT TWO WEEKS** of school left, and Mai wants to cut class today. She wants to go hang out at Daddy Joe's restaurant. "And get something good to eat."

"You coming?" she asks me.

We standing out front of the school, watching everybody else go in. Talking to Ming while Ja'nae is braiding his hair.

"Y'all going or not?" Mai asks.

Ja'nae ain't going. She's scared her grandfather will find out and she'll really get into trouble.

Ming tells Mai she better take her butt to class. "'Fore you get shipped off to California sooner than you want."

We ask him what that's supposed to mean. He says

Mai's gotta go live with their father's people for the summer.

I make this face, like I smell something rank. "You gonna be living with Koreans?" I ask Mai. "Just you and all of them?"

Mai bends down and plucks Ming upside the head. That hurts. I can tell by how red his face is now.

"If you wasn't my sister . . ." he says, balling up his fist.

"Man, you can hit sisters," Sato says, walking over to us and bobbing around like he's in a boxing ring. "You just can't hit girls outside your family. But sisters, they always got it coming to 'em."

Ming slaps him five. Says Mai's getting on their parents' nerves. "So she's gotta go," he says, ducking. Mai pops him again. "Anyhow," he says, looking over his shoulder at us. "My father says it'll help her figure out who she is."

Mai gives Sato and Ming the finger. Then points to her tattoo. "This is who I am."

Ming shakes his head. "She hates Koreans. Hates 'em, and she's one too. Now do that make any sense?" He stands up. Grabs Mai's arm and presses it to his. "You know what, Mai?" he says, pushing her away. "You ain't a hundred percent nothing. So get over it."

Ja'nae tells Ming to chill. I tell him to get off Mai's case. "And just let her be who she wanna be."

Ming says I should mind my own business. Then he turns to Mai and says something to her in Korean. *"Ni-gah noo-go in jial myun, pal-eh-gah ahn ssuh do dweh jah nah."* I don't know what it is, but it makes Mai cry. Next thing we know she's across the street, all up in this boy's face. He's new to our school. So quiet, we call him Q.

"We better go talk to Mai," Ja'nae says, putting Ming's hair in one big braid and telling him she'll finish it later.

Ming ain't happy with Ja'nae. He says he ain't thinking 'bout Mai 'cause she's always mad 'bout something. Ja'nae keeps walking. "We all like sisters," she says. "So I gotta go."

I don't want to go over there 'cause Zora just got off the bus. She's headed Mai's way.

I stay behind a minute and ask Ming what he said to Mai. He rubs his forehead. "I said, 'If you really knew who you were, you wouldn't have to write it on your arm.'"

Ming walks off, not even saying good-bye. I head for Ja'nae and Zora.

"Hey," I say to Zora in a tiny little voice.

She don't speak to me, but she got a whole lot to say to Ja'nae. She asking her what's up with Mai. Then says Ja'nae needs to talk to Ming and get him to stop being so mean to Mai.

"It ain't all Ming's fault," Ja'nae says. "He likes being mixed. He don't know why she don't."

Mai puts her hand out for another tissue and asks if we gonna go to Daddy Joe's with her. Zora says we can count her out.

Ja'nae puts her arms around me and Zora. "Go. So you and Raspberry can make up."

I tell Ja'nae I ain't mad at Zora. Zora puts her purse over her shoulder. Folds her arms and says that I should just go ahead and tell 'em what I did. "Then they'll know why we're not friends anymore."

Mai and Ja'nae look at me like I'm gonna tell 'em the truth. I don't. I tell Zora to tell 'em. I'm scared, though. 'Cause she just might. Only she ain't done it so far, and I don't even know why.

Zora shakes her head no.

"Is it about your dad and her mom?" Ja'nae asks.

"Or your real father?" Mai says.

Zora says she ain't telling. "Because my telling won't make it any better."

I roll some of Miz Evelyn's quarters around in my

pocket. I ask Mai if she's still going to Daddy Joe's.

"Yeah," she says, throwing her tissue in the grass. "Maybe we can do something tomorrow, Zora. You, me, and Ja'nae."

Zora says she'll ask her dad to take them to the movies. I'm glad, 'cause maybe when he don't see me there, he will drive by our place to ask why. Then Momma and *me* will get to spend time with him—to do something special, like drive around for ice cream or go see a movie.

The three of them make plans for the weekend. I sit by the curb waiting for Mai. *I'm never giving Zora her money back*, I say to myself.

# CHAPTER SEVENTEEN

**THEY NEED TO SHUT DOWN** Daddy Joe's. I tell Mai that when I see a smashed-up roach on the floor by the booth we sit in. She's laughing. So is Sato. It's me and Q that look like we want outta here.

"When you have food, you get roaches," Mai says. Then she starts talking about how her family's food truck got a few of 'em too.

"You can get shut down by the government for that," I say, wiping my hands on my shorts.

Q unzips his backpack. Pulls out watermelon-flavored hand gel. Squirts some on his hands. Mine too. Sato says we all just pathetic. "A few germs ain't gonna kill you."

Mai's shaking her head, but she got her hands out too.

Daddy Joe's is exactly sixteen bus stops from our school. On Saturdays the place is hopping. People line up outside all day long to get a table. During the week, things slow down. Like now. There ain't nobody here but us four and two tables with one person each at 'em. We in the restaurant ten minutes before anybody comes from the back and asks us what we want.

"I ain't got no money," Sato says, looking at me.

I roll my eyes at him. "I got money," I say, "but I ain't buying you nothing."

The waitress is so neat and pretty you wonder why she works in a place like this. "Don't waste my time, now," she says, staring at Sato.

"Give me . . . Give me a bag of chips and some iced tea," Q says. "Vanilla pudding too."

Mai orders apple pie, a glass of water, and french fries covered in gravy.

"Help a brother out, Q," Sato says, trying to get money. "I'll pay you back. I get paid Saturday."

"I got your back," Q says, trying to sound cool.

I check out the dead flies hanging on the dirty yellow strip in the corner. I stop counting at fifteen.

Q's dipping his barbecue chips in his vanilla pudding one at a time and smacking his lips like that mess taste good. Sato's getting down on cheese fries and milk. I'm sitting with my hands folded in front of me. Sato puts a fry up to my mouth and tells me to taste. I shake my head no. But I eat the fry anyhow.

"Q," he says, "you know Raspberry is so cheap that she don't spend money on her own self? Not a dime," he says, sticking another fry in my mouth.

I chew on the fry real slow, trying to make it last. Q wipes his bowl clean with his two middle fingers. He tells Sato that he don't know that much about me. Mai tells him that I'm the cheapest girl in the whole wide world. We stay in that place three hours. The waitress finally asks us to leave when she sees we ain't doing nothing but taking up space.

Sato and Q leave us as soon as we get outside. There's a basketball court up the street. They say they gonna walk ahead and check it out. Me and Mai take our time. I ask her about her dad. Whether he's really gonna send her away or not.

She stops. Grabs hold of her long, thick hair and says, "If he makes me go, I will cut it off. Snip, snip, gone."

My eyes get big. "Your dad will kill you."

"So?" she says, rolling her eyes. Next thing I know

Mai's jumping over a fireplug, her long hair flying all over the place.

"Now, that's what I like: a Puerto Rican girl with long pretty curls," some boy says. He's mowing grass in front of the funeral parlor without no shirt on. The blond hair on his chest looks thick and wet, like the stuff you take off corn when you clean it. He looks older than us. Like seventeen or eighteen.

"*Hola*, little momma," his friend says. "Won't you come to Poppa?"

Mai fingers her tattoo and keeps on walking.

The boy with the hairy chest crosses the street and follows us. "You too good to speak?" he says.

We walk a little faster.

"*Señorita*, will ya please-a tell me your name-a?" he says, keeping up behind us and putting his hands in her hair.

Mai pushes his hand away. He pulls on her hair again.

"I'm not Puerto Rican. I'm black," she says, stopping and pointing to her tattoo.

He laughs. Says she should wear a bigger sign if she wants people to know what she really is.

I look him up and down and tell him he needs

a sign himself. *"Stúpido,"* I say, remembering some Spanish.

Mai starts saying stuff too. *"Idioto."*

I slap her five, but the words that come out his mouth next shut us both up.

*"Perpetrator,"* he says. "That's what you should have on your arm. Your forehead, too," he says pointing there. *"Fake."*

Mai crosses her arms and says, "I said I'm not Puerto Rican."

Sweat is dripping down the side of his face. He takes his T-shirt and wipes it. Smells the shirt and makes a face. "Well, you ain't black, neither. Not all the way, anyhow."

Mai puts her arm next to his. His is almost as dark as hers. "How you know what I am?" she says.

He laughs. "I got eyes," he says, sticking his neck way out. "Two of 'em."

I can see Sato and Q up the street about a block and a half away. I tell Mai we should go 'cause they gonna wonder what happened to us. The boy with all the lip starts walking away, telling Mai she could say she was Puerto Rican if she wanted. "Those girls are hot," he says.

Mai and me start walking again. "See what I mean? People think they can say anything to me," she says, digging in her purse for a rubber band and putting her hair in a ponytail.

"He was just talking," I say, sitting down on the curb. "Don't pay him no mind."

Mai says she already forgot about him. But she don't say nothing to me, Sato, and Q the whole time we're on the bus headed back to school. When Sato asks her what's wrong, she doesn't speak. But before we off the bus she hands me a note. *Why do people care what I am, anyhow?*

I write her back. Smack Sato's hand when he tries to snatch the note from me. *I don't care if you black, white, or crazy, even. We girls. All the time.*

She smiles—a little. Writes me back and hands me the note while we stepping off the bus. *I'm black. I'm black*, it says, like maybe she won't believe it herself if she don't keep repeating it.

# CHAPTER EIGHTEEN

"**T**RUTH OR DARE?" Zora says, pointing to me.

I act like I don't know what she's talking 'bout. So I go over to the table in the corner of the basement and sit by myself. "I ain't playing that game."

School's finally out for the summer. We're at Mai's house. She tricked me. Said it was gonna be just her, me, and Ja'nae. I show up and they got Zora here, too. Mai and Ja'nae want us to make up. "'Cause y'all not being friends is making it bad on all of us," Ja'nae says.

I don't like this game. I told 'em all that from the start. But everybody else wanted to play truth or dare. So I went along, too. Now I'm sorry.

"Don't play, then," Zora says, getting mad.

Ja'nae comes over to me. Whispers in my ear, and begs me to be nice.

I tell her it's not just me not talking to Zora. "She ain't talking to me, neither."

Mai is lying on the couch, eating black licorice. She waves a piece at me and says, "You did something to her, that's why."

I ask her why she told me to come if she gonna lie on me. Zora rolls her eyes at me and says she's gonna go home.

"Come on, Raspberry," Ja'nae says. "Play."

We supposed to be at the movies, but Mai's mom ain't got back from the food truck to take us. "I don't wanna play this game," I say, getting up and going over to Mai. I dig my hands in her bag and take three licorice.

"Greedy," she says, snatching a piece out my hand.

Ja'nae wanted to play cards, but Zora don't know how. Mai wanted to watch TV, but ain't nothing on. It was Zora's idea to play this game. I think she wanna show me up with it. Ask me something that's gonna embarrass me.

"Let's do hair," Ja'nae says, fingering her braids. "I need to get these redone. Y'all can take 'em out for me."

We tell her no. Then before I know anything, we back to playing the game. They dare me to call Ming and tell him I hate his guts. Ja'nae ain't going for it. She snatches the phone from me and starts telling Ming not to believe nothing I say. Then she asks for Sato. When he gets on the phone she says, "Raspberry likes you."

I stick my licorice down her skirt, snatch the phone, and throw it on the couch. Zora's laughing. Mai is too.

"Truth or dare?" Mai says, starting the game up again. "Ja'nae's mom's coming to live with her."

Everybody's eyes are on Ja'nae. She's smiling like crazy. "True," she says.

Zora drinks the last of her iced tea. "But she's crazy. She lives in somebody's basement, doesn't she? Trying to heal people."

Ja'nae's mom went to the store when Ja'nae was little and never came back. She lives in California. And every now and then she and Ja'nae sneak and call one another. Ja'nae's grandparents don't like it, so I don't see how they letting her mom come live with them, even though it's their daughter.

"You sure?" I ask Ja'nae.

She doesn't want to talk about it now. She points

to Mai. "Truth or dare? Did your dad change his mind about sending you to live with your cousins in California?"

Mai's eyes get big. She's jumping up and down. Running 'round the room like them people on TV when they get picked to play on a game show. "You mean I'm not going? I'm staying here? All right!!"

Ja'nae tells her she better not tell Ming who told her that. "He said your mom talked your dad out of it."

When Mai points to me and says "Truth or dare?" I don't get mad that it's my turn again. I figure Mai's truth or dare wasn't a real one nohow. So mine is gonna be easy. "Did you take money out Zora's purse? Truth or dare?"

Zora smiles. Ja'nae won't look at me. She's playing with Ming's gold baby ring. The one she wears around her neck. Mai asks the question again.

I walk over to the steps. "I ain't no thief."

Ja'nae comes over to me. "Just give it back. Say you sorry so we can be like we was before."

I tell them they was wrong for doing this to me. Mai says they know how much I like money. "Too much, sometimes."

"But you ain't a bad person," Ja'nae says. "Not a real thief," she says, patting my back.

Before I think about it, I'm digging in my pocket and pulling out quarters and dollar bills. "Here," I say, holding it out to Zora. "Take it."

Mai does a little dance. Ja'nae hugs me tight from behind.

Zora never looks up. And her voice never changes—it's still slow and sad. "We might be sisters one day. That's what my dad said about me and you just before your mom got hurt." Zora stands and heads up the steps. She tells me that she got mad at her dad when he said it. Because him and my mom are so different. "But I changed my mind, when your mom was in the hospital. Daddy cried that night. I heard him, after you went to sleep."

I walk up the steps. "Zora . . . here . . . take it. Please," I say, clearing my throat.

"I didn't know the money was gone for a while," she says, shaking her head no, when I push the money her way.

Ja'nae's yelling for us to come back downstairs. Zora's in the living room, telling me that in her family, stealing is like killing. "My father says that when you steal from somebody, you kill their trust in you."

Change falls outta my hand. I stop to pick it up, and I apologize for what I did.

"You need to tell my dad what you did," Zora says, opening the door.

My hands start to shake. "No. I'm not," I say, afraid to look Zora in the eye.

Zora shakes her head and opens the door. "You know what, Raspberry? You're a thief and a liar, just like your dad," she says, walking out.

Ja'nae and Mai come upstairs when they hear the door slam shut. "What happened?" Ja'nae says.

"You took the money back, didn't you?" Mai asks.

I ball my money up, put it in my back pocket, and open the door wide.

"Don't go!" Ja'nae yells.

I move as fast as my legs can go, and try hard not to think about what Zora said. But her words come into my head anyhow, and before I'm at the corner, I know she's right . . . I'm just like my dad.

# CHAPTER NINETEEN

Ja'nae TELLS ME TO STOP walking so fast. "It's hot. And
your legs are longer than mine."

I slow down, and ask her again if she thinks I'm
like my father.

She takes her time answering. "I guess not."

I like Ja'nae more than the rest, 'cause she will
stick by you no matter what.

"When you took the money from me that time,"
she says, pulling up her long skirt, "I ain't have to ask
for it back. You felt bad, and just gave it to me. Even
though I owed it to you."

I don't want to talk about the money, even though
I can't get Zora's words out my head. So I ask Ja'nae
how come she ain't tell me 'bout her mother coming

here. She kept it to herself, she says, 'cause she ain't know if it would really happen or not. "Anyhow, everybody is mad at everybody else. Or mad at somebody else that done something to 'em. I just decided to keep it to myself."

All the shades are down in Ja'nae's house. So she's going from window to window pulling 'em up, letting in the light. She's talking on the phone to Ming too. Telling him to come over. "My grandfather ain't coming home till late."

She hangs up the phone and drags me from the living room to the kitchen. Her grandmother went to California to bring her mother back. So she's gotta cook dinner for her grandfather for a week. She's pulling out frying pans and pots; washing off chicken breasts and whole potatoes.

Ja'nae flours the chicken and puts it in a pot of hot bubbling grease. "Set the table. Four plates."

I tell her I don't wanna eat with her grandfather. She looks at me and smiles. "Sato's coming."

I stink. My hair is frizzed up from the sweat and heat. "I don't want him here."

Ja'nae comes over to me. "You scared he might kiss you or something?"

I make her get her chicken fingers off me.

She laughs. "We just gonna watch TV."

While the chicken is frying and the potatoes and pork and beans are cooking, Ja'nae and me running 'round the house picking up newspapers. Then Ja'nae hands me a blue spray bottle and a rag. "We have to do the bathroom."

"That's your toilet, not mine."

She asks me if I want my chicken smelling like the toilet. I take the rag and tell her she gotta pay me if she want me for her maid.

"Take it outta Zora's money," she says, trying to be funny.

I don't say nothing to her. But all the while I'm cleaning, I'm thinking about Zora's money and how hurt she was back there.

Soon as we get the table set and the food in pretty bowls, the bell rings. It's Ming and Sato.

"I know you saved me some food," Sato says, coming into the house all loud. He don't even say hi when he walks in the door. He just walks right into the living room, sits down like a cowboy getting on a horse, and starts digging his dirty fingers into the biscuit bowl.

Ja'nae is like her grandmother, pushing all kinds of food Sato and Ming's way.

Ming says he ain't hungry. Sato piles chicken and potatoes on his plate like this is his last meal. After we done, I ain't so sure telling them two to come over was such a good idea. Ja'nae and Ming are hugged up together over there on the couch. We're watching a scary movie. Every once in a while, Sato leaves the room and comes back another way trying to make Ja'nae and me scream.

In the middle of the movie, Ming shuts off the TV. Puts on a CD and starts dancing with Ja'nae. It's a slow song. They're dancing so close you couldn't get a notebook between 'em.

"Want to?" Sato says, pulling my arm.

I push him away. "No!" I say. "I mean. Hmmm. Cut the light on, Ja'nae. I can't see."

Ja'nae ain't listening. She's giggling over there with Ming.

Ming moves her over my way. Drops some of Ja'nae's sweet-smelling cotton balls on my head and says, "Don't be scared. He ain't gonna hurt you."

Sato is standing in the middle of the floor with his hands in his pockets. "I'll show you how to do it," he says, real low. "It ain't hard."

I ain't never danced with a boy before. But I ain't telling Sato that. So I sit on the couch like a knucklehead, wishing I was home with Momma.

# CHAPTER TWENTY

**B**EFORE JA'NAE AND MING finish dancing, I'm out the
front door and headed for home. I hear her yelling for
me not to be like that, but I keep on stepping.

By the time I'm at the end of the block, Sato is
walking beside me. Matching every step I take. We
don't say a word to each other till we get to the corner
of Nectar and Oak—four blocks away. We in trouble
too. The fireplug is on full-blast. Water is shooting
halfway 'cross the street onto passing cars, and kids
and grown-ups are standing in the street trying to
cool down from the heat. Sato and me don't move.
We staring at wet women sliding barefoot across the
slippery street like it's made of ice. We laughing at
the pigeon-toed little boy pulling off a wet Pamper

and sitting down on the curb butt-naked. It's crazy. Everybody and everything is wet, except me and him.

After maybe ten minutes, a man yells for somebody to hold back the water so me and Sato can pass. Six little boys stick their butts up to the fireplug. The water squirts up in the air like a fan.

We halfway 'cross the street when one kid holding back the water says, "Now!" You can't outrun water. So we don't try. We get soaking wet, like everyone else. After that, Sato pulls me over to the fireplug. He holds me 'round the middle while he stands right behind me making sure the water soaks every part of me. I'm kicking and screaming and laughing— swallowing water and wiping it out my eye with my fist. I'm pulling at Sato's wet, slippery fingers, and begging the girl next to me for her bucket.

"It's so hot, you don't mind people trying to drown you," Sato says, walking over to the curb and sitting down with me. A few minutes later, he's talking about what happened at Ja'nae's.

"How come you ain't wanna dance with me?" he asks.

I lean over and let the cool water roll over my hand. "I don't know."

Sato asks me again. I tell him the truth this time. He don't laugh. He says he only slow danced two other times before. "I was practicing with my aunt the first time."

Momma probably been home from work a long time now. So I'm gonna be in trouble when I get in. But it's like a party out here. Water and music and food everywhere. Nobody hurting nobody else. Just people having fun.

I squeeze water out the bottom of Sato's T-shirt.

"You like your freckles?" he asks.

I stare down at my wet, wrinkled shorts. "I don't know," I say.

He looks up the street at a man pulling a woman into the waterfall. "I do," he says, sweet and low.

I keep my mouth closed after that, 'cause I don't want to ruin things.

By the time we get to my place, my hair is dry and crunchy like Brillo.

It's almost eight o'clock. Sato and me been saying good-bye for a long time. But we still here, in front of my apartment building. I'm standing on the second step. Sato's on the pavement. There's a bunch of kids over at Miracle's building making all kinds of noise.

They got a lamp on the porch, and they playing cards and eating food. Weave Girl ain't with 'em. So nobody's paying us no mind.

"I gotta go," Sato says again. "I'll be in trouble if I don't."

"Me too," I say, looking away when his eyes fix on mine. I wonder, when he licks his dry lips, what it would be like to kiss him. Not a long kiss, like they do in the movies. Just a quick one. *A peck*, Ja'nae would call it.

Then I see Odd Job coming our way.

"Raspberry Merry."

I back up two steps. "You better go," I say under my breath.

Odd Job elbows Sato in the side. "You don't know how to call and say you gonna be late?" he says to me.

"Man," Sato says, pointing and laughing at me. "Your mom sent Odd Job to find you? That's so lame."

I sit down next to Odd Job. He says Momma called him from the university and told him I wasn't home. Asked if he could go look for me.

The three of us sit out front for twenty more minutes before Odd Job says for me to get inside so he can go take care of his business.

I walk up the steps backward, saying bye to Sato six times in a row.

"You got a home, ain't you, boy?" Odd Job says, putting Sato in a headlock, and knuckling him on the head.

Sato is so embarrassed. "Aaah, man. I ain't like that," he says, breaking loose from Odd Job's big, strong arms. "Raspberry's the one that be trying to come after me," he says, walking up the street backward. "Ask her. See if it ain't true."

Odd Job looks at me and winks. "Better stay away from her, boy, 'fore I have to cut you or something," he says, reaching in his pocket like he gonna pull out a knife.

I turn to Odd Job and tell him to stop it.

"Oh, so you embarrassed now," he says, walking up the steps. "Good. That's what I'm here for."

We sit on the top step till Miracle's friends get so loud we can't think.

"Let's go," he says, but neither of us moves.

I close my eyes and breathe. "Don't they smell pretty?" I say about the flowers.

Then I tell Odd Job how Sato wet me up in the fireplug, and how he is the first boy ever to say he likes my freckles. Odd Job leans back on the step and looks me in the eyes. "You sure are pretty," he says.

I smile, and wonder when Sato's gonna say something nice like that to me.

# CHAPTER TWENTY-ONE

**I**'M SLEEPING IN TODAY, even though I could be at work with Momma making money at the dry cleaners. Her boss wanted somebody to come sweep up. Momma asked if I wanted to do it. I said no. I'm too tired. But I was lying. I just wanted to stay in bed and think about Sato. Wonder what it would be like if him and me went together. Momma asked if I was sick, turning down money. I told her no. Just tired.

After Momma left, I went back to sleep. Ain't wake up until two o'clock in the afternoon. Stayed in bed eating cereal out the box and watching movies until four. Then somebody knocks on our front door right when my show's getting good. I'm so busy trying not to miss nothing that I open the door without asking who it is.

"Raspberrry!" my father yells with his arms stretched out. "Give me a kiss, girl."

I take a giant step backward, and try to shut the door. "You can't come in. Momma said so."

Daddy's run-over boot keeps the door from slamming shut. "I don't want nothing," he says, "just my visiting rights is all."

Daddy's high again. He's gotta hold on to the door to stand up straight. "You okay?" he asks, pulling the door wide open, then letting out a big breath, like he just hauled trash to the curb.

I tell him that I'm okay. But I'm not. My insides feel like warm Jell-O. I gotta squeeze my lips together so what's in me don't come up and go all over him. I swallow and feel sicker inside.

Daddy's nose is running like it's cold out. He wipes it with the back of his hand, rubs his fingers down his pant leg like he's fixing a crease. "Your momma in there?" he says, peeking behind me.

"Yeah. No. She's coming in a minute, though," I say, hoping that'll scare him.

Daddy's friend is sitting on the steps, holding his head in his hands like he's trying to keep it from falling off. A big, brown water stain covers the back of his white T-shirt. Tiny lint balls, looking like popcorn pieces, are stuck in his hair.

Him and Daddy smell—sour. I hold my breath. Turn away when I see greasy black marks on the back of Daddy's neck when he asks his friend if he got a headache.

I hated it when Momma and me lived on the streets. The worst part, though, was not being able to wash up when we wanted. We smelled sometimes. Or itched from dirt stuck to our skin like crumbs. When Momma and me was out there, we washed up at restaurants and gas station rest rooms. But sometimes we couldn't get to one for a few days. That's when I missed having our own place, being able to clean up, like real people.

I look at the brown stuff under Daddy's nails and the dried blood on the side of his face. "You need a bath, Daddy," I whisper, opening the door wider. The words come out my mouth at the same time my brain is saying for me to run inside and find another hiding place for my money.

"You Daddy's girl, all right," he says, pushing past me. Yelling for his friend to come in and get something cold to drink.

Right away, I know I done the wrong thing. 'Cause, soon as he's inside, Daddy's sitting on the couch with his boots up on the coffee table—his friend's opening the fridge, taking out chicken and Kool-Aid, bread and mashed potatoes.

"You a angel, girl," his friend says, sticking his finger in the potatoes and sucking it. "Sent from heaven, I tell you."

I'm sitting on the floor, under the window. I can smell Momma's flowers. They make it seem pretty in here, even though it ain't.

Daddy goes into the kitchen, opens the fridge, and takes out a peach. He sits down on the other end of the couch and smiles. "You getting big," he says, not trying to stop the juice from sliding over his lips and down his chin. "Pretty, too. The boys looking at you yet?"

I start smiling, like I'm stupid. He asks for the boy's name. Says for me to tell Sato he will kick his butt if he breaks my heart. That makes me feel good for a minute, till I realize that this is Daddy and he don't never mean what he say.

Daddy rolls the peach seed around in his mouth. Pulls it out with his fingers and says he's gonna plant it in the park where he lives sometimes. "Grow something pretty, like your momma does," he says, sticking it in his back pocket.

His friend hands him a plate with two chicken sandwiches on it, piled high with lettuce and tomatoes. They don't say one word to me while they eating. I excuse myself. Head for my bedroom to get my money, till I get to thinking real good that they might follow me in there and take it all. So I go back to my spot under the window. Sniff the flowers and the funk, and hope Momma calls soon to check in on me.

Daddy crosses his legs and passes gas. "That was good, good, good," he says, picking food out his teeth with his fingers, then laying down on the couch.

"You can't stay," I say, standing up. "Momma's gonna . . ."

He says they ready to leave any minute now. But they need to wash up. I go to the bathroom. Come back with washcloths and towels. Soap, too. "You first," Daddy says to his friend. And while the guy's in the bathroom, Daddy tells me how they're both broke. "Ain't got a penny between the two of us."

I'm in the kitchen, putting food back in the fridge, so worried 'bout them taking my stash that I'm dropping forks and napkins, tasting warm Jell-O in my throat again. "We broke too," I say, bending down and wiping mayo off the floor.

Daddy smiles. Says he gotta pee. I'm glad, 'cause

now I can go put my money someplace else. Drop it out the window into the yard, even. But when I get into the living room, I see Daddy in Momma's room.

"You ain't supposed to be in here," I say, snatching her jewelry case out his hand.

"Y'all got a little change? A few dollars, don't you?"

I shake my head. Tell him again to get out. "Now!"

He ain't listening. He's opening drawers. Checking dress pockets and dumping out old purses Momma got piled on top of a shelf in her clothes closet. I run out the room. Grab the phone and start dialing Momma's job.

"Your momma just gonna get mad," he says, pressing the receiver down. "She'll call the cops or something."

His hand is covering mine. Rubbing and squeezing my fingers at the same time.

"Just a few pennies. Ten, twenty bucks. Your momma got that 'round here someplace, don't she?"

If I say yes, and go get him a little cash, he will leave—maybe. But if I say no, he will stay way too long, begging me for money, maybe even hurting me. So I nod my head up and down and tell him not to follow me when I go get the money.

"Whatever you say, princess."

Momma always keeps a few dollars in her room. But I can't give that to him. It ain't right. So I go to my room and get the money I took off Zora. Before my hand is out from under the rug, though, Daddy's got ahold of my money. Pulling back the rug and taking a whole bunch more.

"That's mine!" I scream. "I worked for that!"

I ain't notice how red his eyes was before. Or the way he keeps licking his lips and clicking his teeth. "It's a whole lot here. Maybe two hundred dollars," he says.

"It's mine," I say, trying to grab it off him.

Daddy slaps my hand. "How you get all this money, girl? You stole it?"

I tell him I ain't no thief. "So give it back."

He's walking into the living room, hollering for his friend. Asking me again how I got all this money. "'Cause if you stole it, then you had this coming. 'Cause nothing good comes of bad money."

I get up in his face. "Then you shouldn't take my money, 'cause nothing good's gonna come of it," I say, holding both my hands out.

Daddy's friend opens the front door. He asks how much Daddy came up with. I beg my father again and again not to take my stuff. He looks me right in the eye and says, "Sorry. But I need this for something."

When he's outside on the pavement, I let out a scream so loud and scary that Miz Evelyn across the street comes to her front door and asks what's wrong.

"They," I say pointing to my dad. "They . . ."

My father pulls down his pant leg and straightens up his back. "Nothing good's gonna come of it nohow," he says, shoving the money in his pocket and walking away.

I can't move. It feels like my feet are stuck in ten pounds of peanut butter. But I scream so much that Miz Evelyn runs into the street, right in front of a moving car, just to get to me.

"You all right," she says, holding me. Rocking me. "No matter what, you gonna be all right."

I know what she says is true, but I cannot stop screaming. No matter how hard I try.

# CHAPTER TWENTY-TWO

Momma nailed the windows shut. All of 'em. She said she would pick up three ceiling fans and that would be enough to keep us cool. I tried to tell her that we was gonna die in here with no outside air to breathe and cool us off. But she ain't listening to me.

"He might come back while I'm working and hurt you, or take everything we got," she said, banging nails into the wood, closing her eyes when paint chips start to fly.

It's my fault, what happened. I told her that. But Momma ain't hold it against me. Just said she wanted me safe. After that she got on the phone with Dr. Mitchell and mentioned something about getting a restraining order against Daddy. That way the police would pick him up if he came around again. I was for it, at first. I ain't want him taking no more money off me. Then it made me sad thinking of them hauling him off to jail. Momma musta felt the same way, 'cause by the time she was done on the phone, she decided not to do it. But the nailed windows was gonna stay shut, she said. That was a week and a half ago. I been sweating ever since.

Yesterday Momma came in my room real early, before the sun was even up. "We gotta get outta here," she said, laying down next to me. Holding me so tight it hurt.

I was wondering when Momma would say it was time for her and me to hit the streets again. To live anyplace but here, where Daddy can find us anytime he wants. I turn my head, so she don't see me cry.

"No, baby," Momma says, wiping my tears. "We ain't running, just getting away for a while. To the beach. Like rich folks do when they can't take it no more."

Momma said she talked to Dr. Mitchell late last night. Told him she needed to get away to someplace pretty. I wanna stay here, I tell her, and make back the money Daddy stole off me. Momma says no. I gotta go too.

"I'm not frying up chicken or packing a thing,"

Momma says, crawling out my bed. She's wiping sweat off her neck with a shirt I got sitting on the dresser. "I'm just gonna have fun, for once."

Zora and me are in the backseat. She's pressed up against the door like she's trying to get out. I'm leaning on the other one. We both facing a window, so we don't have to see or talk to each other.

Since my dad stole that money off me, I keep thinking about what Zora said at Mai's house. She's right—even if I don't say it to her—when people steal, they kill something deep inside you.

By the time we stop for gas, and pick up chairs and new towels, it's loud and crowded on the beach. The sun is white hot and the blue in the sky is as pretty and clear as the dish liquid we keep in a bottle by the sink. The sand is so hot you can't just walk on it. You gotta run or hop from foot to foot to get across.

Momma says for me and Zora to go find a spot. She and Dr. Mitchell gonna rest. Zora and me both do the same thing—look around at all the shiny, greasy people sitting in lawn chairs and lying on the sand. "We not gonna find a good spot," I say, with my hands on my hips. "It's too many people out here."

Dr. Mitchell tells me and Zora to get going.

"Unless you two wanna stand up all day." Then he and Momma start taking off their clothes. Folding 'em, and laying 'em over the chairs. "We'll be in the water," he says, taking Momma by the hand and running.

Me and Zora stand there like we stupid. She picks up a chair and Momma's things, and starts walking with her sneakers in her hand.

"Your feet will burn," I say, before I remember we ain't speaking.

Her gray eyes find mine. They look soft and sad. She drops her sneakers in the sand and steps into 'em. Then she picks up her bag and chair and keeps walking. I do the same.

The spot we find is too close to the water. I tell Zora that.

"So sit someplace else," she says, flapping her beach towel too close to my face.

I move my stuff away from hers. Sit down in the chair and watch Momma and Dr. Mitchell. He's trying to make her go into the deep part of the water. Momma can't swim. She's pushing him away and laughing real hard.

I roll my eyes at Zora. "Excuse me," I say, snatching my magazine out from under her foot.

Zora rubs sunscreen on her arms and legs. When she gets her CD outta the bag, sand flies into my face. I blink and rub my eyes and tell her to watch it.

"*Now* you know how it *feels*," she says.

I know she ain't talking 'bout the sand, neither.

"I hope he stole *all* your money," she says, hopping around on the hot sand. "Just like you stole mine."

I stand up and walk over to her. Put my left foot on top of my right one. "You got plenty more left," I say.

Zora pulls at her swimming suit straps. She's fed up with me, I guess. "I'm gonna tell my father, right now, how you stole money from me," she says, standing on one foot, and rubbing sand off the other.

I wanna tell Zora that it don't feel good having somebody you know take what's yours. But she's running for the water. "Don't tell," I say. "Don't tell on me!" I say as loud as I can. But she's in the water. Swimming. Standing by her dad. Pointing my way.

# CHAPTER 23

I DON'T KNOW WHY ZORA ain't tell on me. But she didn't. If she had, Dr. Mitchell woulda said something, or treated me different. When he got out the water, he pressed his wet hands on my back and asked if they was cold. Then he winked at Momma and pulled me into the water. Him and me swam all the way out to the roped-off part. Zora stayed back on the sand reading magazines and drinking pop.

By the time we get home, it's late. People next door are out playing cards and loud music. Zora's asleep in the backseat, so Dr. Mitchell says he ain't gonna come in the house. He drives off once Momma and me go inside.

"I think my back is sunburned," Momma says, looking over her shoulder.

I go to my room to pull my swimsuit off, watching wet sand fall to the floor in clumps. I tell Momma it's hot in here and the fans ain't helping none.

"Go to sleep and you won't notice," she says, turning the shower on. A half hour later she comes in my room wet all over and smelling like oranges. "Cut the lights off," she says, yawning, bending over and kissing me good night. "I already locked the front door."

Momma's snoring fifteen minutes after she leaves my room. I ain't ready to go to sleep, so I take a shower too. It don't help. As soon as I'm done, sweat is running down the side of my face, soaking my shirt and the back of my shorts. I take a butter knife and try to open my bedroom window. The knife bends all the way over, but it don't open the window.

I go to Momma's room and answer the phone when it rings. It's Dr. Mitchell. He's not calling for Momma. He's calling for me. When we were on the beach, he says, Zora told him that I wanted to talk to him. "But not with your mom around. So that's why I'm calling now."

I almost pass out.

"Something wrong, sweetie? You in trouble or something?"

I tiptoe outta Momma's room. "No. She musta made a mistake."

Dr. Mitchell's in the kitchen. I hear the microwave going. "Zora says it was really important. Something bad."

I open the front door. Sit out on the steps.

"Is it about your dad?" he asks.

I fan myself with my hands. "No."

I wish Dr. Mitchell would hang up the phone. He won't. He's still trying to find out what happened. Saying he'll get it outta Zora, then.

I don't want Dr. Mitchell to be disappointed in me and leave me and Momma. So I lie to him. "It's, it's Miracle. The girl up the street," I say, peeking to see if she's out. My voice gets low. "She's still bothering us."

He asks what she's doing. I can't think of nothing. So I make more stuff up. "She said she was gonna kick my butt if I didn't give her some money."

Dr. Mitchell goes off. He says he's coming over tomorrow and talking to her. That he wants Momma there too, 'cause they need to put an end to all the crap from her and "that Shiketa."

I'm on the pavement, walking back and forth. Chewing my nails and wondering why I keep making things worse.

"It's okay, Dr. Mitchell. Miracle, ummm, said she was sorry. Right when we came back from the beach she apologized."

I ain't sure he believes me. But he quiets down. "If anybody, *anybody* messes with you or your mom," he says, "call me."

A cab pulls up to Miracle's building. Miracle gets out wearing a long white gown, like maybe she was in a wedding.

Dr. Mitchell says he's going to bed. But before he hangs up, he asks about me and Zora. Why we not talking. I do what Zora did. I don't tell the whole truth. "It's partly her fault, partly mine. But we back to being friends now."

When he hangs up, I go back inside. I fix a bowl of cinnamon flakes and watch TV. Then Zora's words pop in my head like answers to a test. *You're a thief and a liar, just like your dad.*

I don't get mad when I hear the words this time. 'Cause I know they true.

# CHAPTER TWENTY-FOUR

**I** **DIDN'T WANT TO TELL ON MOMMA,** but I had to. Our place is burning up. My hair stinks all the time 'cause it's so hot in here. When I woke up this morning, my bed was soaking wet. Wasn't no talking to Momma, 'cause she had her mind made up. "The windows's gonna stay nailed shut for good."

Odd Job says I did the right thing, calling him up. "Both y'all gonna end up in the hospital if she keeps this up," he says, walking through the place with a chisel and knife. Busting the nails and pulling the windows wide open.

Momma tells him it ain't none of his business what she does in her place.

"My place. I'm the landlord. This is my building.

And you can't nail the windows closed, 'cause if they find you two up here dead, they gonna say it was me that offed you."

Momma don't think that's funny. I do. "Smell the flowers, Momma," I say, going over to the window and sniffing.

Momma's walking from room to room, picking up paint chips. Telling Odd Job Daddy's gonna break in here for sure, now that the windows ain't nailed down.

Odd Job takes her by the arms. "He didn't break in. Raspberry let him in. Before that, he walked up to the front door and knocked."

Odd Job goes into my bedroom and comes back with a can. "Okay. I'll drive around the place a couple times a week. I'll check things out when you ain't here," he says, holding the can under Momma's hands. The nails fall to the bottom like pennies in a pot.

Momma looks so scared standing there with her hands out. "It's not just him. It's everything. Shiketa. Miracle. All of it."

I walk over to Momma and put my arms around her. She goes to her room, comes back, and hands Odd Job a letter.

Dear Miz Hill,

They say I should write you. So that's what
I'm doing. Sorry I hit you. Sorry you had to
get stitches. But you shoulda stayed out my
business. Anyhow, I'm gonna do community
service when I get out. Right round the corner
from my old place.

Odd Job tells Momma she needs to show the letter to her lawyer. To tell 'em she don't feel safe with
Shiketa communicating with her. Momma hands him
another letter.

Dear Shiketa,

I hope you never get out.

Momma's crying. Saying she don't know why she's
writing such mean things to Shiketa. "A child."

Odd Job pats her back. Lets her know that she
got the right to be mad over what happened. Momma
presses wrinkles out her dress with her fingers.
"Nail up the windows," she says, reaching in the can
and pulling crooked nails out. "If we don't nail the

windows shut, he's gonna come back. She will too."

I look at Odd Job. Then at Momma. This ain't like her. She's always strong. Always knows just what to do. "Mail the letters, Momma. Let her know how mad you are at her and then maybe you won't be so mad and sad inside."

Momma won't look at me. She's at the window with the hammer. Banging nails. I go over and reach for the hammer. Odd Job pulls me away.

"Hit it," he says, raising his hand. "Bash the window in, if you want. Smash a hole in the wall," he says, pulling Momma's hand back and aiming for the window.

When glass smashes and falls to the ground like frozen water, we all look at each other like we don't know who did it.

"Sometimes it's better to be mad all at once," he says, "not in little bitty pieces that leak out of you like oil from a busted tailpipe. That happens, and you never do get over it. Just stay sad and miserable all the time."

Momma bends down to pick up the glass. She says she'll quit her job at the dry cleaners to be home with me more. I don't want her to do that. We need the money.

"Raspberry can work for me. Make some extra change, you know," Odd Job says, sitting down on the couch.

Momma drops glass into the trash can. "I don't know."

Odd Job's voice gets low. "When we lived in the projects, your mother took my mother and me in, when hard times hit. She let us stay there three whole years."

Momma's crying again.

"I'm always gonna look out for you and yours."

I pick up the hammer. Odd Job winks. I take that thing and slam it into the glass.

# CHAPTER TWENTY-FIVE

"**H**EY, REDS. I LIKE IT," a boy says, making an outline of my body with his hands. When I look his way, he blows me a kiss from the window of a shiny black car with tinted windows and big silver rims. He tells me to come talk to him a minute. I shake my head and turn away, but I can feel my cheeks burning.

"You growing up, all right," Odd Job says, staring at the boy. "Guess I need to be calling you plain old Raspberry, huh? Not Raspberry Cherry and stuff like that."

We left Momma back home cleaning up and waiting for the glass man to come by. Me and Odd Job going to the bank, then out to eat.

Everybody knows Odd Job, so we get stopped six times before we even get to the bank.

When we walk into Goodies Restaurant, Odd Job opens the door and lets me go inside first. "Any boy that don't open the door or pull out the chair for you ain't worth your time," he says.

"Boys my age don't care 'bout stuff like that."

Odd Job don't wanna hear that. "You gotta make a boy treat you the way you want to be treated. But first," he says, opening up the menu, "you gotta know how you want to be treated."

I don't wanna talk about boys with him. So I change the subject. When the waitress comes, Odd Job asks me what I want to eat. I order waffles.

"Me too," he says, licking his lips. "But make mine three orders of three each. Bring me a bowl of blueberries and plenty butter." He stops the waitress when she turns to walk away. "How 'bout a order of bacon, some eggs, and a large orange juice, too."

The busboy over at the other table keeps staring my way. I don't take my eyes off the fork and knife till my food comes.

"The boys treating you all right, ain't they?" Odd Job asks.

"Why you wanna talk 'bout that stuff?" I say, putting my napkin in my lap.

Odd Job says he just noticing how the boys are

looking at me. "Especially Sato," he says, smearing butter on his waffles and toast. "You like him, huh?"

I'm playing with the food on my plate.

"You like him or not?"

I smile. Try to eat a piece of bacon but I can't stop grinning. "He's all right."

When we're done eating, Odd Job pulls out his cash. "A gentleman always pays for a lady's meal," he says. "And leaves a tip. You know a brother is cheap and triflin' if he eats and don't give the waitress her due when he's done."

I look at him, wonder why he's telling me all this. When we get back outside, Odd Job asks me if I miss my father.

I belch and keep walking.

"When your father was in his right mind, he treated your mom like she had golden feet and diamond eyes," he says, letting out a belch, too.

We walk for blocks not talking to each other. Then Odd Job says he seen Daddy, not too long ago.

I stop walking. Press my fingers to my lips and close my eyes. "He ain't coming back, is he?"

Odd Job's big brown arms cover me. His muscles bunch when he squeezes me tight. "He ain't stealing from you no more," he says. "Me and him talked about that."

I wipe my eyes and look up at his. They are burnt-toast brown and got long red lines shooting through the white parts, like he's way past tired. "You get back my money?" I ask.

Odd Job turns me loose. Starts walking again. Says he woulda got my dough, but wasn't none of it left by the time he caught up to Daddy.

I ask if he went looking for him. Odd Job don't say yes or no. Just that he put the word out that Daddy better stay clear of Momma and me.

We almost back at Odd Job's spot when I ask him if he would ever hurt Daddy. He don't answer, just says can't nobody do nothing worse to Daddy than he already done to hisself.

He's right, I guess. But I can't help wondering what Odd Job said or did to Daddy to get him to stay away from us—for good.

# CHAPTER TWENTY-SIX

**F**INALLY, SOME GOOD NEWS! We moving into that house in Pecan Landings. Momma went to the hearing today and the judge told those people who live around there that he will hold them in contempt of court if they try to interfere with us moving in. Momma says we can move in right away. Today is July 1st. We moving in there one month from today.

I'm thinking about this while I'm sitting out front of our place talking to Mai and her cousins. They're headed for the market not far from here to buy some ginger. "My dad says it's cheaper at that store," Mai says.

This is the first time I'm meeting her cousins. The little one says her name is Ling. She's six years old. Short and cute. Got long, straight black hair down to her navel. Crooked front teeth and blue eye-glasses shaped like stars.

Ling's sister is named Su-bok. She's thirteen and really pretty. Her hair is short and spiked high on top. It's black, but the tips are as white as glue. I don't know what her eyes look like 'cause of the sunglasses.

Mai asks if I want to go with them to the store. I lock up the house first and try to make conversation with Ling while we walk. She act like she ain't got no tongue. She hunches up her shoulders or shakes her head no when I ask her something. When we get to the store, Mai says for her and Su-bok to wait outside with the dog. They brought it with them from California.

"They make me sick," Mai says, smacking her forehead with both hands. "Every chance I get, I ditch 'em."

When we walk up the cookie aisle, Mai opens a package of chocolate sandwich cookies. The kind with thick, white cream inside. She looks up and down the aisle and pulls out four of 'em. "Here," she says, handing me two. I shake my head no. She shoves two into her mouth and two into her pocket, slips the package back on the shelf, then starts walking real fast.

I ain't never seen Mai take what wasn't hers before. I tell her that, too. She rolls her eyes. Says it wasn't stealing. "Just sampling. That's all."

Mai is walking up and down every aisle, even though we already got the ten bottles of ginger she came for. She keeps talking about her cousins. "Since they came, people stay on my case," she says, pulling out a cookie and stuffing it in her mouth. "We went to a Korean grocery store yesterday and the owner gave them free cookies and gum. Su-bok had to *make* him offer me something. I told him to keep that crap."

Mai wipes black crumbs off her lips, then hands the cashier the money. We walk out the door and up the street. Su-bok and Ling trying to keep up, but Mai and me moving so fast, they end up half a block behind. I make Mai stay put so they can catch up. When they do, a boy sticks his head out a car window, starts speaking gibberish and pointing to Su-bok. His braids are undone and his hair is all over his head. "Hey you. You," he says, pointing to her. "Come here. I got something to ask you."

Mai takes the last cookie out her pocket and throws it at him. It bounces off the car and gets smashed to pieces when the tire rolls over it. "See?"

she says, walking fast. "See what my father did? Made everything worse." Then she takes off running.

Su-bok snaps her fingers and moves her hips to music the rest of us don't hear. "Evil," she says, pulling up her sunglasses and staring at me. "Mai is evil."

I don't say nothing.

"She wakes up mean, goes to bed mean, and is mean in between." She laughs. "Hey, that rhymes."

Ling stoops down and hugs her dog, Couch. They call him that because he lays on the couch all the time at home. Then she takes her fingers and pulls his lips back, trying to get him to smile.

"It doesn't bother me," Su-bok says.

I look at her, wondering what she talking about.

"The way people stare. That doesn't bother me. I just figure they think I'm cute."

Su-bok takes off her shades and sticks them in her back pocket. Except for the brown of Mai's skin, and the crinkles in her hair, them two look almost the same—even their teeth are shaped alike.

We stop at a corner store and get something to drink. The boy whose father owns this store never pays me no attention. Now, he is sweet as pie. Saying "Thank you" and "Yes" for no real reason at all. Putting our stuff right in a bag, not asking me if I want one or not, like he usually do. I see him making eyes at Su-bok. I don't care. I hate him anyway.

Su-bok takes Ling's hand when we cross the street. "Where I live in L.A., there's all kind of boys: Black. Chinese. White. Hmong. Mixed. Mexican. Korean. Shoot," she says, holding out her hand so she can take a sip of my pop, "around my way, a girl can have a different color boyfriend every day of the week. Nobody stares. Nobody cares."

Mai is waiting on my steps when we get there. Su-bok ain't in no hurry, though. She stops on the corner. She says she wants to check out the boys. Ling races the dog to the house.

"You like it here?" I ask Su-bok.

"I like the boys. They're cute. They ask for my phone number all the time," she says, smiling. "At home, my father is strict. Watches everything I do."

I ask Su-bok if she speaks Korean. She says yes. They have to speak it at home. We're on my front steps now. Couch is across the street lying on a sofa somebody put out for trash last month. Ling is with him.

Su-bok pulls loose strings from her shorts. "Ling and my father sit and talk Korean all day long," she says, standing and waving to some boys who are breaking their necks to check her out. "In one way I'm like Mai," she says, "English is good enough for me. *Comprendes?*" She laughs.

The three of us sit here for a while. Then Mai says it's time to leave. Before she takes off, I ask how her lessons are going. Su-bok answers for her. "She has to spend one hour a day speaking Korean with me and Ling."

Ling looks both ways before she crosses the street. She sits on Mai's lap and traces her tattoo with her little fingers. "Can I get one of these?" she asks.

"You ain't black," Mai says.

Ling looks like she don't know what Mai's talking 'bout. "A little bit. I have to be a little bit black, if you're my cousin. Right?" she says, staring at her arm.

Su-bok reaches her arms out to Ling. "I'll get you a tattoo. One for little kids. The big ones hurt. Right, Mai?"

Mai looks down at her arm. "I guess," she says, standing up to leave.

# CHAPTER TWENTY-SEVEN

**F**IRECRACKERS. That's what Odd Job's got in his hands when he knocks on our front door.

"Ain't they illegal?" I ask, picking up a long, skinny red one, and rubbing some of the powder off. "People lose their eyes and fingers all the time with these things."

Odd Job squeezes my nose. "Party pooper," he says, heading for the refrigerator. Pulling a tub of no-name ice cream out a green plastic garbage bag and putting it in the freezer.

"The Fourth of July without fireworks is like cake without ice cream. Useless," he says, heading back out the door and down to the backyard.

I go to my room, open the window, and sit on the ledge with my legs hanging out. It's nine o'clock at night, and our party is just getting started. Momma calls it our It's About Time Something Good Happened to Us party, in celebration of the new place we're moving to.

Our yard looks like one of those department store windows. Momma's got red Christmas lights strung along the inside of the wooden fence; circling our tree and twisted around some of the branches. Long thin poles with cups of fire hanging from 'em are stuck in the ground. Red, white, and blue Christmas bulbs are stacked in clear plastic bowls on three tables she borrowed from Miz Evelyn. And all the people who come in get a red, white, or blue shooting star drawn on their cheeks in glitter paint by Ja'nae.

We ain't never had a party before. But people are gonna be talking about this one forever. Momma cooked up a storm. Grilled chicken, burgers, and hot dogs. Made potato salad, fruit salad, and a tuna mold shaped like a cat. Mai's mom brought over egg rolls and fortune cookies. Dr. Mitchell went to the bakery and brought cakes and pies. Me and Ja'nae made lemonade, iced tea, and Kool-Aid. Sato brought over six cans of warm red pop, but I didn't crack on him. It's the thought that counts.

I swing my legs just over my window ledge. Feel

the hot air blow over me. Close my eyes and smell the lavender blooming like crazy all over our backyard.

Ming and Ja'nae are sitting by the fence, pointing up at the fireworks that the city just set off. Odd Job is playing spades with his girlfriend Donyell, Momma, Dr. Mitchell, Ming's mom and dad, Su-bok, Ling, and Miz Evelyn from across the street.

Sato and Ling are playing with Couch when Sato points at me and says, "I'm coming up," with Couch following behind.

My bedroom is a mess. You can see dirty socks, jeans, and T-shirts shoved under my bed from when Momma told me to clean up earlier. But I don't try to straighten things now. I reach over, dim the lights, and hope Sato don't trip over nothing.

Couch licks my fingers when I pat his head. Sato sits down next to me. "Man," he says, pointing up at the sky, "why can't we have fireworks all the time?"

I nod my head up and down. I look over at him and see red and white lights in his eyes just when more firecrackers explode way up above us.

Sato tells me to move closer to him, then he puts his arm around my shoulder. I look down to see if Momma's watching. She's busy showing Ja'nae her plants. Odd Job's busy telling Dr. Mitchell that

148

he needs to stick to doctoring 'cause he sure can't play no cards, so them two ain't paying me no attention, neither.

Sato asks me about Zora. How come she ain't here. I tell him she's at her mom's for the weekend. Her mother's planning a trip to London and Zora gets to go.

Sato's sitting so close to me I can't even look up, or I'm gonna be staring right into his nose. So I swallow, then clear my throat, and wonder if my breath stinks.

We sit there, stiff as the poles holding the fire in the backyard. Then he leans over and tries to kiss me. I turn away, and ask Couch if he's hungry. "For some ribs or barbecued chicken," I say, rubbing his tail.

Sato leans over. "All those flowers your mom planted," he says, pointing around the whole yard, "make it look like your yard don't even belong around here," he says. "Like somebody stole it from Pecan Landings and is hiding it here."

My eyes follow his fingers. I smile when I see the row of orange begonias I planted by the fence the other day, and the pink, white, and red rosebushes that been growing like crazy all summer. "That bushy thing that looks like weeds is lavender," I tell him.

"And the blue stuff over there crawling all over the fence is morning glory."

Sato takes my hand and points to a corner of the yard with tall things growing in it. "What's that?" he asks.

But he tricks me, and before I can answer him he kisses me—right on the lips—just like Ming and Ja'nae. I ain't never been kissed before.

When I open my eyes, he's staring straight at me.

"Your eyes is supposed to be closed," I tell him, kicking my legs out like I'm high up on a swing.

He's smiling. "Why?"

"Because."

"Well, I like mine open," he says, taking his arm from around my shoulder and holding my hand.

I kick my feet out again. "Who you kissed before?"

He rubs the little hairs over his lip. "Just you," he says soft and low.

I feel his fingers cover mine, and his lips get close again. My heart is tick, tick, ticking in my chest. My head is spinning, for real, from the sweet smell coming from the cologne on his neck and the flowers in the yard.

"Sato! You crazy, boy?" Dr. Mitchell says, just when Sato's soft lips touch mine again.

Sato stares down, then over at me, then down into the yard again.

"You! Down here! Now!" Momma says, jumping up from the table. Shaking her fist in the air.

Everyone in the whole yard is staring up at us. "Busted!" Ming yells out.

"Man!" Sato says, helping me off the window ledge and holding my hand all the way to the front door. I stop him in the vestibule. "They gonna jump all over you," I say, talking 'bout Momma, Odd Job, and Dr. Mitchell.

"That's all right," he says, looking me right in the eyes. "You was worth it."

# CHAPTER TWENTY-EIGHT

**B**EFORE **S**ATO EVEN GETS one foot in the backyard, Odd Job grabs him by the arm and says he needs to talk to him a minute. Momma got me over here in the corner saying that it's not right for a girl to have a boy in her room. "I know you think it was only a kiss," she says, tucking my hair behind my ear. "But remember, you are just fourteen. There will be plenty of time for things like that when you're older."

I tell Momma that she can trust me. Then I go over by the bushes near the fence, close my eyes, and remember how good it felt being kissed by Sato.

"Sato's your boyfriend," Ling says, sneaking up on me. Reaching out her arms so I can pick her up.

Dr. Mitchell is minding my business again.

Pinching Ling's cheeks, and saying, "Raspberry's too young to have a boyfriend."

"She kissed him. Like this," Ling says, taking off her glasses, pushing her lips out, then pressing 'em to my cheek so hard it hurts. "Ouch," she cries, holding her mouth. "I bit my tongue." She tells Su-bok she wants a Band-Aid.

Su-bok is with Ja'nae and Ming. "You don't need a Band-Aid, Ling," she says, coming over and looking inside her mouth. "Stop bugging me."

"You say mean things, just like Mai," Ling says, squeezing my neck tight.

When Sato walks over to us, Ling almost jumps outta my arms trying to get to him.

He got his arms stretched out to her, but his eyes on me. "Don't fall," he says, yanking her by the corn-rows Ja'nae put in two days ago.

Su-bok takes a swig of soda, then says she wishes Mai was here.

Mai is on punishment for smart-mouthing her dad again. Su-bok stands up on a crate, and looks over the fences at Miracle and 'em. They been hanging out there for the last three days. Partying half the night. Setting trash cans on fire and playing music so loud

Momma almost called the cops. I asked Momma not to say nothing to 'em. To just let us move from 'round here and not think no more about 'em. She said that wasn't hard. She was tired after all that nonsense with Shiketa. "Besides. I gotta think about you. I'm not here all the time. Don't want Miracle starting up with you while I'm gone."

"Hey. Cops," Su-bok says.

Ming tells her to move over and he stands on the chair behind her. Sato just opens the gate. "To get a better look."

Momma's inside with Odd Job and Dr. Mitchell getting more food and ice. So we all sneak out, even though Mrs. Kim and Miz Evelyn say we shouldn't. It's Miracle, in trouble again. Some boy is holding her hands behind her back. Telling her to cool down 'fore the cops haul her away. When she sees me, she goes off. Starts cussing. Asking us what we looking at. She's yelling at me, saying she still gonna kick my butt for getting her girl put away.

Ja'nae's the one who says we need to get Ling back inside. Ling keeps asking what the girl did wrong. None of us answer her.

"Hey, Miracle," Sato yells. "You gonna need a miracle to get outta this one."

I pop him on the head, and ask him if he trying to get me killed.

Momma comes out front too and so does Dr. Mitchell. He's standing behind her with his arms wrapped around her waist. "A young girl like that, what does she have to be mad about all the time?" he says, taking Momma's hand and pressing it to his cheek.

We all walk back inside after the cops settle Miracle down and tell her she better make sure she don't find no more trouble tonight.

Momma tells all of us to get a glass or can of something 'cause she wants to make a toast. "To good times . . . and good friends," she says, holding her can of red pop up in the air.

Ming's got his right arm wrapped around Ja'nae's neck. He touches her glass with his, then to mine and Sato's too. "Yeah," he says. "Here's to all that stuff you just said."

At midnight, we set off the fireworks. Ja'nae, me, and Ling hold hands and run around the yard in circles holding sparklers high in the air. When mines burns out, I go get another one. Sato's right behind me, whispering. "I liked it . . . kissing you."

I take a deep breath. I look at all the pretty lights in the yard, and listen to everyone laughing and talking. "Me too," I say loud enough for even Momma to hear.

# CHAPTER TWENTY-NINE

**I**T TOOK US ALL WEEK to clean up from the party. That's okay, though, 'cause I ain't never gonna forget how much fun I had. Ja'nae and 'em are still talking about it. Asking me when I'm gonna get off punishment for kissing Sato. I tell 'em that I don't know. Momma ain't saying just yet.

It's different now, between Sato and me. When we at Odd Job's, he stares at me all the time. I can feel his eyes on me even when my back is turned. Every once in a while, Odd Job grabs him by the ears. "I ain't paying you to stare at Raspberry, boy. I'm paying you to work." Then Odd Job comes over to me and smiles. "Now you done ruined him for good," he says. "His mind used to be on work, now it's on you. Might have to fire that boy."

I tell Odd Job not to do that. Sato is making money so he can give some to his mom. "It ain't his fault—"

"That you're so pretty," Odd Job says, pulling me by my hair. I wore it down today. It's sticking to my neck, itching me in all this heat. But Sato says he likes it this way.

Sato's soaking wet with sweat. On our way home, he stops by an open fireplug and sits down under it. His sneakers bubble up every time he takes a step. "Feels good," he says, squeezing water from his shorts while we walking.

I'm trying to think of something to say to him, but words won't come out my mouth. All I do is smile. All he does is stare at me, then look at the ground. A few blocks away he stops and points. "Ain't that your dad over there?"

My heart starts pounding. I look up. There he is, sitting on the curb. Leaning against a big plastic trash can. Legs spread wide open. Head down. No shirt. No shoes. *No shame*, I think.

"That cop's gonna bust that bum's head wide open," some man says, like he just can't wait for it to happen.

I look over and see a cop car pull up, lights flashing.

"I hope he don't crack your father *one* with that nightstick," Sato says to me.

"Let's go," I tell him. But my feet ain't moving.

Sato takes my hand. "Maybe he's hurt or something."

"Drunk, or trying to come down from that mess he been taking," I say. "You staying? I'm not," I snap.

We start walking. Sato's still looking back at Daddy.

"Get up," the cop says to Daddy. "You can't stay here."

Daddy starts throwing punches. Out comes the nightstick. Next thing you know, the cop whacks him upside the head. Blood runs down the side of his face.

"Don't hit my father!" I scream, running over to him.

"Girl," another police officer says, holding my hand up in the air, "you better calm yourself."

I'm not afraid of him. "He's sick. Why you hitting him just 'cause he's sick?"

Daddy's blood is so dark it almost looks black. It's all over the place. On his shorts. Dripping onto the concrete. Squished between the gloved fingers of the other cop trying to cuff him now.

I bend down and whisper in his ear. "Daddy. It's Raspberry. You hear me?" I say, taking the tip of my shirt and wiping blood out his eye.

He lifts up his head and looks at me with one eye. "Hey, baby girl."

The cop pulls me by the arm. "This your father?"

I nod my head yes. Watch another cop car pull up to the curb, lights flashing.

"Well. You can visit him at County. He's going to jail."

Traffic on Madigan Street ain't hardly moving. Everybody is staring at us. A man in a gray suit and gray sunglasses yells out his window, "Lock the drunk up."

I look down at the blood on my shirt and my sneakers.

"Raspberry," Daddy says, when they get him to his feet and make him walk over to the squad car. "I love you, Raspberry Girl."

I look at him. He ain't wearing shoes and his feet are black and blistered. My stomach flips. My mouth tastes like acid. Next thing I know, vomit is coming out my mouth and nose. The cop is cursing, saying this is the way his whole stinking day has been going.

I can hear Daddy cursing at the cops, saying to take his cuffs off so he can make sure that I'm all right. They shove him in the car anyway.

Soft, warm fingers start to rub my back and shoulders. Then a woman says for me to relax and just let it all out. "You'll feel better when you're done," she says, handing me a bunch of tissues. She wipes my face and mouth, opens her half-empty bottle of water and hands it to me. I shake my head no, at first. *Germs*, I think. But I take and drink it anyway. Every drop.

The woman walks off and leaves me when another policeman comes over and asks, "Is he really your father?"

I wipe my mouth with the back of my hand. "Yeah," I say, feeling Sato move closer to me.

"Get in," the cop tells me, opening the door. "I'll take you both home."

I look at him. "Home?" I say. "But he don't live . . ."

The cop smacks his lips. "He goes with you or he goes to County. Loitering is an offense. I can lock him up or take him home. What's it gonna be?"

The tall cop is me and Daddy's color, with moles all over his face. He looks hot in his tight, blue uniform. Mad, too.

"Raspberry," Daddy says, begging me. "All I need is a little time to clean up and sleep this off."

I think about my money. How he ain't mind stealing it from me before. "No," I say, turning my back on him.

"Let's go, buddy," the cop says, pushing Daddy.

"Raspberry," Daddy says. "Please?"

My tongue rolls over my teeth and I smash my lips together when I feel myself ready to say for him to come go with me.

"I'm gonna quit. For real I am," he says, staring over at me.

My father has the prettiest eyes when he ain't on that stuff. "They the color of honey, with splashes of green," a lady at the grocery store told him once. They cloudy now, like the eyes of the old, slimy fish they try to sell you at the market, long after they shoulda trashed 'em.

"Momma ain't gonna like you coming to our place," I say, giving the cop the name of our street.

The policeman tells me to get in the car. Sato too. In a few minutes, he's pulling up to our place. He don't even help me get Daddy to the door. Me and Sato do that.

"We coulda locked him up," one of 'em says,

leaning out the car window. "You caught us on a good day, I guess." He laughs. The woman on the police radio starts talking. The siren and lights go on. The car pulls away from the curb and goes up the street real fast—almost hitting somebody's car—trying hard to get off our street.

# CHAPTER THIRTY

**"Y**OU CAN'T STAY HERE!**"** I say to my father.

He's crawling to the top of my bed. Rolling onto his stomach and pushing my hand away when I say he's gotta go.

We just got here, but I already changed my mind about helping him out. Momma's gonna find out and go nuts again. Then she ain't gonna trust me never, no more.

Daddy's head is still bleeding. Blood is all over my sheet, on the floor in my room, and the rug in the living room. I'm walking in circles. Using a wet sponge to wipe the blood off my fingers and from beneath my nails. Telling him again and again, "You gotta go. Now."

He's sleepy. Balled up like a baby with his black feet dirtying up my pink spread.

"Use some gloves," Sato says, carrying the bucket to the bathroom. "You don't know if he has AIDS or not."

We walk back to my room, water spilling over the sides of the bucket and onto the floor. The knot on Daddy's head is as fat and wide as a doughnut hole. His eye is still swollen shut. "It hurts," Daddy says over and over again.

Sato wrings out a wet rag and hands it to me. "He needs a doctor."

I look at him, then back at Daddy. "Doctors don't come to your house," I say.

Sato dips a rag in the bucket, starts wiping the blood away. "You wanna do it?" he says, handing it to me.

I don't blame him. I wouldn't wanna clean him either if he wasn't my dad. "Do his feet then, okay? They so dirty. They look like they hurt."

He puts on a second pair of plastic gloves and reaches for a rag. "Maybe Dr. Mitchell should come."

I squeeze bloody water out the rag. "No. He would tell Momma."

* * *

It don't take Sato long to clean Daddy's feet, even though he had to wash 'em three times 'fore they was mostly clean. And it's easier than I thought to get the blood out the rug. But we can't get Daddy's head to stop bleeding, no matter what we do. In the last hour we changed the bandage three times. Now we gotta do it again.

"He needs stitches," Sato says.

I look down at my gloves. I go to the kitchen for ice, take off the bandage, and ice Daddy's head even though he slaps my hand away when I do.

Sato wipes sweat from his forehead and downs the rest of the pop I gave him. "You shoulda let the police take him," he says.

I look at Daddy and get so mad down deep inside that I want to take something and hit him. *You ought to be taking care of me!* I want to yell. *Protecting* me *from the cops. Not* me *protecting* you. Then I do what I don't want to do. I call Dr. Mitchell. Only he ain't at the office, so I try him at home.

"Your father there?" I ask Zora when she finally picks up the phone.

"No," she says, hanging up.

I call right back. I tell her I really have to talk to

her dad. It's Wednesday, she says. He don't work in the office today. He's making rounds at the hospital. "And you better not bother him there."

I look over at Sato and my dad. "Zora." That's all I can say.

"You finished?" she asks.

"Zora . . ."

I can tell she's gonna hang up.

"Daddy . . ."

"He's not your father. He's mine. So you and your mom stop trying to hog him up like—"

The words fall out my mouth faster than rotten peaches from a wet paper bag. "My father got beat up and the police brought him to my house bleeding and I need somebody to help me fix him up 'cause Momma gonna kill me if she find out he's here."

Zora's so quiet it's like she's not even there. "I woulda given you the money," she says. "Lent you more than that even."

My father turns over, sits up, and coughs. Then goes back to sleep again.

"You supposed to let a person sleep when they get hit in the head?" I ask.

She hangs up the phone.

I look at Sato, then I walk over to my dad and

press cold wet tissues to the knot on his head. The blood still won't stop, so I get more tissue and do the same thing over and over again.

When the phone rings, I tell Sato to answer it. I'm gonna have to call my mother anyway, I think, so it don't matter if it's her on the other end.

"It's Zora," Sato says, handing me the phone.

"You shouldn't let a person sleep too long if they were hit in the head," she says. "You have to wake them up off and on, like they did your mother in the hospital."

I pat my father's cheeks. "Wake up, Daddy."

He turns over and change falls out his pocket— four quarters and a dime.

I whisper the words so low, I ain't sure Zora hears 'em. "I know how it feels when somebody steals from you."

Zora don't waste no time saying what she thinks. "Good. Now tell my dad what you did. Your mother, too."

I wanna let Zora know that this is between me and her—not everyone else in the whole, wide world. But my father starts talking crazy. Saying he wants the money I just stole out his pocket. "I gotta go, Zora."

Zora don't let me hang up before she tries to get

in the last word. "You need to tell my dad, Raspberry."

I put the change back in my father's pocket. "You want me to tell him so he can hate me too?"

Zora don't say nothing for a long time. "Yeah!" she says, hanging up the phone.

# CHAPTER THIRTY-ONE

SATO'S GONE. He said he had to go do something for his mom. Daddy's sitting on the side of the bed, holding his head. Telling me to give him two more aspirin even though he just took four.

"When your mother due in?" he asks, feeling the knot on his head. Looking at his hand and checking for blood.

"Soon," I tell him, glad his head stopped bleeding.

Daddy stands up, zips his pants, and walks over to the chair by the door. I go to my drawer and take out a clean sheet and pillowcase.

"That boy that just left, he that one you talked about liking? Satin. No. Sato, right?"

I tell my father that Sato had to go home. His

mom and dad were going to church and he had to watch his brothers and sisters.

I pull off the bloody pillowcases and sheets and put on the clean purple ones with flowers.

"One day," my father says, wiggling his toes and checking out the bottom of his feet, "I'm gonna send you a case of sheets. Towels too. Pretty ones. Pink. Blue. Ivory."

I go to the window and open it real wide. "You gotta go," I say. "Right now."

Daddy stays put, asking me if I got a comb he can use.

I get loud on him, this time. Ask him how come he don't care if he gets me in trouble with Momma. When he walks out the room, I'm right behind him, making sure he don't go into Momma's room and take nothing. He sits down on the couch, pulls out a pack of cigarettes, and lights up. "When I get myself together, you gonna have more than you need," he says. "Lots of pretty stuff."

I stare down at the floor. "You ain't got no money, Daddy," I say.

My father goes into the kitchen and opens the fridge like he lives here too. Then he says that he ain't always gonna be broke down like he is now. "I'm gonna get me some help."

Daddy's talking 'bout going to a treatment center, and getting his old job back at the office where he worked downtown. I sit down at the table and listen to him go on and on. When he say he gonna buy me a diamond tennis bracelet when times get better, I take my hand and slide it across the table real fast, watching the sugar bowl fly into the air and smash against the refrigerator. Sugar is all over the floor. I apologize to Daddy, then excuse myself and go to the bathroom, taking the cordless phone with me.

"Odd Job," I say, when I dial his cell phone number for the third time.

"Raspberry Merry," he says. "What's up?"

"My . . ."

"You all right?" he says.

"He—"

"He what?" Odd Job says, acting like he wanna punch somebody right now. "Sato done something to you, girl?" I tell Odd Job I ain't want nothing. "Your daddy been by again? He there now? Bothering you?"

I shut the bathroom door. Sit on the stool with my feet and legs up. "My father . . ."

Odd Job says for me not to worry, he's coming over right now. I lie. Say Daddy ain't here. That I heard that he was 'round Odd Job's way yesterday. "I'm just checking is all."

Odd Job tells me he ain't seen Daddy in weeks, then he asks how come I'm talking so funny. "Sad and quiet."

"I just woke up," I say, standing up and unlocking the door.

He says he'll talk to me later, 'cause he's washing somebody's ride right now.

I hang up the phone. When I get to the living room, Daddy's at the front door ready to leave. Wasn't even gonna say bye or nothing.

"Gonna take a handful of your momma's flowers," he says, pointing to the ones out front. "Just to sweeten me up some," he says, sniffing under his arms and making a funny face. Then he tells me how the peach seed he planted is growing real nice. And that one day people gonna be glad he lived in the park, 'cause they gonna be able to eat some sweet, juicy peaches 'cause of him.

I look up and down the street to see if anybody's out. Miracle's sitting on her steps.

"You saved my life, baby girl," Daddy says,

holding my face with his hands. "You my own little angel."

I look down at his feet. Ask where his boots went to. He says he sold 'em, for a "little something, something." But he'll have some soon, 'cause he's headed for the corner right now, so he can hustle up some change.

I pull up the flowers for Daddy and give him more than I should.

He sticks them in his shirt pocket. "I named it Raspberry, you know."

"You named what Raspberry?" I ask, keeping my eye on Miracle.

"My peach tree. I call it my Raspberry Girl."

Daddy walks up the street, stops at Miracle's place like he knows her, and gives her some of his flowers. A few minutes later, he gets up, looks back my way and waves, then walks up the street.

Miracle don't stomp on the flowers like she did before. She don't get smart with me or come over to our place. She's just sitting there watching Daddy walk away, just like me.

# CHAPTER THIRTY-TWO

**H**E DID IT AGAIN. Stole my money while I was in the bathroom, I guess. Most of it wasn't there, though. I put it in the bank like Momma said. But I had a hundred fifty bucks under that rug. And he took it. Just like before. After all I done for him.

"You stupid," Ja'nae says. "Shoulda kept it in your pocket or banked it. Anyhow, he's a crackhead. They always taking what's not theirs."

We in my room with the door shut. Momma's on the phone, seeing when the new beds, kitchen, and dining room sets she ordered gonna be delivered to our new place.

I tell Ja'nae I'm gonna get my money back. "No matter what."

She says it's been a week since Daddy took the

money, so it's spent by now. I don't care. He's gonna give it back to me even if I gotta stand on the corner next to him while he begs for it, I tell her. Ja'nae says that's mean, what I just said. "But it ain't right for your father to take what's yours. To steal from his own blood."

I ain't tell Momma about it this time. I took the sheets, gloves, and rags and dropped 'em in the alley behind Miz Evelyn's house while she was next door talking.

"We going over Ja'nae's house," I tell my mother. She waves her hand and keeps on talking to the person on the phone. She's happy, I guess, 'cause we can buy new stuff for once. Not have to use leftover furniture like usual.

"We gotta hurry up," I tell Ja'nae, when we get to the end of my block. She says she don't want to go. I tell her she can stay here if she wants. But I'm gonna get my money back from my father—now. A half hour later, we getting off the 27A, standing outside Ming's house, ringing the front doorbell.

"Why you gotta drag them into my business?" I ask Ming when Su-bok, Ling, and Couch come out the house with him.

Ming says Mai's on punishment again, and he

gotta watch out for Su-bok and Ling while his parents take her to some counselor.

Su-bok's hair is bright pink today. "What's up?" she says.

Sato is carrying Ling. Her hair is French braided with lots of yellow, blue, and green barrettes. "Ja'nae made me pretty," she says, smiling.

I tell Ming he messed things up by bringing The Cousins. "I can't just take them anyplace. They gonna be scared."

He looks at me like he wants me to be quiet.

"We going to Freejack Park. That ain't no place for kids," I say.

"If Ming don't go, I don't go," Ja'nae says, holding tight to his hand.

"They don't go, I don't go," Ming says, looking at The Cousins.

"All y'all make me sick," I say, walking away from them.

We walk in twos for the next ten blocks. Ja'nae and Ming are first, The Cousins, then Sato and me. He got me by the hand. Every once in a while, I feel his thumb rub my sweaty palm. It's hard to be mad while he's doing that. Hard to concentrate on Daddy too.

In a way, I know what I am doing is stupid. My money is gone, just like everybody says. But I still wanna see my father. I want him to look me in the eyes and tell me how a person can steal from his own child. When we get to the park, Ming starts to back out. He says he might get in trouble bringing his cousins to a place like this. I look at him. His face is as brown as a gingersnap cookie now that the sun's been beating down on it all summer long. His hair is braided all over and pulled back into a ponytail that goes way past his shoulders. He could pass for a Puerto Rican around this way. But The Cousins, they are who they are.

Ain't no kids in this here park. Just grown-ups. Men playing craps over by the wall where the closed-down swimming pool is. Men sweating and cussing while they playing hoops and drinking beer. Women scratching, and taking drags off cigarettes and weed. Crackheads and drunks all over the place.

"I don't see your dad. Let's go," Sato says, pulling me by the arm.

I point to the other side of the park. "He could be way over there, can't tell from here, though," I say, bending down, then standing on my tiptoes, to see what I can see.

Ja'nae lets Ming's hand go. She comes over to me and says, "We shouldn't be here."

I stare into the park, feeling sorry for the trees that look as skinny and half dead as the crackheads walking around here.

"I want to go home," Ling says, putting her arm around my waist.

Su-bok is so quiet. She ain't shaking her butt 'round this place. She all up under Ming and Ja'nae.

"Y'all can go," I tell 'em. "I'm gonna find my father."

"Ahh, man," Ming says, getting mad. "You and Mai get on my nerves. Never listen to people when they telling you the right thing to do."

I look at Sato, wanting him to take up for me. He's staring into the park. "Every week, somebody dies in this here place."

"Everybody goes or nobody goes," Ja'nae says, putting her arm around my shoulder. "We girls. So I gotta go," she says, staring at Ming.

Ming says something in Korean. Ling and Su-bok laugh.

"Oh, Ming, I'm gonna tell on you," Ling says, taking her fingers and digging 'em into Couch's ear.

He growls at her, then walks over to me and lays down by my feet.

"Couch will bite if I tell him to," Ling says.

Sato looks at me like I ain't got good sense. "Let's just go and get it over with."

# CHAPTER THIRTY-THREE

FREEJACK PARK IS SMALL, so it don't take no time to get through the whole thing.

"I can jump rope," Ling says, closing her eyes, turning her hands, and jumping up and down. "One. Two. Buckle my shoe. Three. Four—"

"We don't wanna hear no more," Sato says, picking her up and sitting her on his shoulders.

Ling is laughing. Sato is running with her up there, saying he ain't responsible if she falls down and busts her head wide open. He is maybe twelve trees ahead of us now. Then all of a sudden he stops, turns around, and runs back to where we are. Ling is bumping up and down on his shoulders like she riding a horse, holding on to her eyeglasses. Sato can't hardly talk or breathe when he gets back to us. "I seen, I seen your father. Over there," he says, bending down and letting Ling off.

Warm Jell-O fills my mouth again.

"You okay?" Ja'nae says, taking my hand.

I nod my head yes.

Sato gets all up in my face, his breath smelling like milk. "He don't look so good. Maybe you don't wanna . . ."

I don't plan for it to happen, but my feet start moving backward. Sweat starts running down the middle of my back like ants crawling down my spine.

Ling grabs my other hand. "How come your father lives outside, Raspberry? Not in a house with you?"

My mouth is so dry it hurts when I talk. "He just don't, that's all," I yell.

Ja'nae tells me to stay put till we can think of what to do. The ants are on my legs and arms now. I'm sweating and itching everywhere.

Sato is talking about the sun going down and us not being in here when that happens. I look up at the sky. It's as bright as it was first thing this morning. It's only seven o'clock at night, I want to tell him. The sun ain't going no place.

Ja'nae is talking and talking. Saying that even

though my father ripped me off, he is still my father.

I look at a man wrapped tight like a mummy in a greasy, green sleeping bag, and a woman with no hair pushing a shopping cart full of trash.

"I wanna go," Ling says, starting to cry.

Su-bok says she ain't scared, but she's holding on to Ming's shirtsleeve.

My feet start up again. And we all walk past the swings with no seats, rusted monkey bars, and seesaws with half the seat broken off. Sato says Daddy is over there. I run to where he is and holler at the top of my lungs, "Give me my money back!"

My father is covered with old newspaper. His eyes open and shut. Half a smile is on his face.

"Had a bad night," his friend says, covering his eyes from the sun. "He can't hear nothing you say."

I put my hand out, and tell him I want my money now. His friend laughs. Says whatever Daddy took off me is long gone now. Then he tells me I better get going. "Your dad would be mad at you being in a place like this."

I push away the newspapers. Dig in his pockets. Tell him over and over again he ain't have the right to take my stuff. "To steal what I worked for."

"Raspberry," Ja'nae says, coming over to me.

I take both my hands and shove my father good, trying to make him turn over so I can check his back pockets. "You got it. I know you got it!" I say.

Sato and Ja'nae pulling me by the arm. Saying we need to go. My father still ain't awake, and Ling is crying so much I think she gonna be sick.

"No! No! I ain't leaving till he gives it back," I say. "All of it."

Daddy's friend digs in his pockets and pulls out the insides. "We broke, girl. Don't you see that?" He stands up, smelling just like he did in the hospital. "And if we get us a quarter, we gonna go get more stuff. 'Cause that's how it is."

I back up. Look down at my father, snoring. "Where's his tree?" I ask.

Ja'nae says I'm crazy. "There's trees everywhere."

Daddy's friend points to a tiny little plant near their bench. Rocks are circling round it. A big, flat stone is laying on the ground next to it with "My Little Raspberry Girl," scratched on it, in big crooked letters. I throw the stones outta my way. Lift my foot high in the air and squish the plant with my sneaker.

# CHAPTER THIRTY-FOUR

**WE GETTING OUT THIS PLACE TODAY.** Moving to Pecan Landings. Momma is so happy. Me too, 'cause finally we gonna be living someplace nice, where bad things don't happen to you all the time, and Daddy won't be able to find us. So, August 3rd is a day I'll never forget.

Our house is full of people: Dr. Mitchell, Odd Job, The Cousins, Ming, Ja'nae, Zora, and Sato. Mai is on punishment *again*.

Ja'nae's got a cherry Popsicle in her hand. Sweet, sticky juice is dripping down the side of the stick and running over her fingers.

Zora is over by the fence, talking to Sato. She ain't said one word to me all morning, even though I spoke to her three times. Dr. Mitchell made her come help out. Said he had enough of our nonsense. But you can't make people be friends, I guess. So she's here, but it still ain't no different between us.

"Help me carry this," Ja'nae says, licking her fingers and looking down at a big box of plants Momma pulled out the ground yesterday.

I'm looking around the yard. It's a mess now with holes in the ground from all the plants me and Momma dug up, and bags full of junk we ain't want to take with us to our new place.

"Raspberry. Let's get going, girl," Momma says, walking over to me. "Everybody's working but you."

"Okay," I tell her. But I don't move. I stand on my tiptoes and look over the fence. Watch Miz Evelyn sitting out on the porch in a long white robe. Momma already said good-bye to her. I want to, but I can't.

"Stop playing around, girl," Sato says, pulling the back of my hair when he walks by.

I open the fence. Walk out to the pavement and sit out on the curb. Ling sits next to me.

"Mai likes living in Pecan Landings," she says.

I smile and look at Miracle's place. "I ain't gonna miss being here," I tell Ling. "Not one little bit," I say, standing up and going back inside.

It takes us three more hours to finish packing.

After we done, we stuff ourselves in Momma's car like too many vegetables in a crisper. Ling steps on my foot and tries to push my legs out the way so she can sit by Sato too. Momma looks back and tells her there ain't no room. That she needs to get in Odd Job's car. Ling's got her mind made up, though. She squeezes her little butt in between me and Sato, then starts whining that it's too tight back here.

"Get out, then," I say. But it don't matter. Sato sits her in his lap. Ling pokes out her little pink lips and kisses him on the cheek.

By the time Momma gets in the car, we all sweating and Ling is crying 'bout something else.

"Miz Hill, where's the air?" Sato asks. "You got a new ride so I know you got some air in here."

Momma slams the door shut. Turns to him and says, "Soon as I start driving, you're gonna have all the air you ever wanted. Your window's down, right?"

Everybody laughs. Momma says for us to wait a minute, then goes back inside and gets pop for all of us, even the people in the other cars.

"Let's go, Miz Hill," Ja'nae says, hanging out the window. She's in Dr. Mitchell's ride with Zora, Ming, and a whole bunch of clothes and boxes.

Zora's sitting up front. She got the visor down

and she's staring at her eyes. She don't take the drink, like everybody else in the car, or answer Sato when he stick his head out the window asking who she getting pretty for.

"Let's go!" Odd Job shouts out his car window. Then he beeps his horn. Dr. Mitchell does too. Su-bok reaches over Momma and presses down her horn. We drive right behind each other off the street, beeping our horns nonstop, yelling out the windows and waving tissues and socks like we in a parade. I look out the back window and see Miracle sitting on her front steps. She's glad we're leaving, I bet. Me too.

Our place in Pecan Landings looks brand new. The landlord repainted it inside and out. He replaced the stove and refrigerator. Dr. Mitchell, Momma, and me went over there and repainted my room though. It's blue with stars on the ceiling, just like Momma and me always talked about. When you cut the lights off, the stars glow in the dark.

After we unload everything, all the kids sit down and do nothing. Momma gets on us to unpack some things.

"We tired, Miz Hill," Sato says, laying on the

living room floor next to me. "This here is hard work."

Momma says we have ten more minutes to rest. If we don't get moving then, everybody better just go on home and leave things to "Raspberry and me."

I tell them to get busy, 'cause I don't want to do all this work by myself.

Momma gives everybody a partner to work with. Naturally, she puts me and Zora together. "Do the basement," she says.

Zora looks at me with them green cat eyes she got on today—they match her shoes and shorts. Then she stomps all the way down the basement stairs. I don't wanna work with her. She don't wanna work with me neither and tells me that. She says just because her father made her come today doesn't mean she likes being here or that we friends again.

I stack Momma's old albums on the shelf, even though we don't have a stereo to play 'em on. Then I ask Zora to help me move a desk, after Momma said it's in the wrong place.

She looks at her nails. "I broke one over at your old place and messed up my shorts," she says. "So you need to get somebody else to help you."

I wanna tell her father on her. To let him know

she don't wanna do nothing but try to look cute. But if I tell on her, she might just tell on me. So I move the heavy desk all by myself. In between wiping sweat off my face and neck, I watch Zora. She could care less about me right now.

I tell Zora I ain't working with her no more. So I go to my room. Su-bok's there all by herself. She's glad to see me and I'm glad I came in, 'cause she's putting all my clothes in the wrong places. I'm dumping out those drawers, telling her how mean and selfish Zora is.

"Ja'nae just told me that you took Zora's money," Su-bok says. Then she tells me how she goes to school with a boy who steals money outta people's lockers.

I snatch my jean shorts out her hand. "I ain't no thief."

She asks if I took Zora's money or not.

I look at myself in the mirror on the closet door. "It's not like that," I say.

I tell Su-bok I don't wanna talk about Zora no more. She starts talking about my dad, then. Asking if I ever found the money he took off me.

"Crackheads don't never give you your stuff back," I say, throwing a box of clothes on the bed.

We don't talk for half an hour. Then Ja'nae comes

in, saying she called Mai on the phone downstairs. "Her mom says the two of them need to get away—alone—and talk about all the things Mai's been going through."

Su-bok stops working. She starts talking 'bout what happened yesterday at the mall when Mai punched a boy.

"Him and his friends were so cute," Su-bok says. *"Nuh-moo nuh-moo gui yoh woh!"*

"What?" I ask.

"Very, very cute," she says.

"Black?" Ja'nae wants to know.

Su-bok puts sunglasses on. "Two black. One white. All cute," she says, sitting on the bed next to Ja'nae. "I gave one boy my phone number. Another boy asked Mai for hers. When she gave it to him, he asked if she was mixed. Ling with her big mouth said that she was part black too, just like Mai."

The boys thought that was funny, Su-bok says. So they started making jokes. Telling Ling that she didn't look black. Asking her to point to where the black was. "My sister is so stupid," Su-bok says, kicking off her sandals. "She starts looking at her fingers and toes. Feeling her face and nose. Saying for Mai to tell them that she *was* black, too, just like her."

Mai flipped. Told Ling she was not black, not even a little, tiny bit. Ling started crying real loud. One of the boys tried to be smart and asked Mai if she was really mixed. 'Cause he "couldn't find no black in her neither."

"Mai popped him in the forehead for saying that," Su-bok says. "I don't blame her."

Zora walks in the room, right then.

I ask Su-bok if she's sorry she came to visit. She says no. She likes all the cute boys we got here.

Zora sits down next to Su-bok and turns away from me.

Su-bok keeps talking. "I go to a private school, far from my neighborhood. It's mostly white. Sometimes I want to scream because people don't get who I am." She's sitting cross-legged on my new blue rug. "They think because I'm Korean that I'm not an American. That I'm supersmart at math and science."

Zora turns to her. "Are you?"

Su-bok laughs. "Yeah, but not because I'm Korean. My stupid father makes me study all night long and take special classes on Saturdays."

Ja'nae asks Su-bok if she talks to Mai about stuff like this. "A little," she says, using my brush on her hair. "I tell her that people don't know what I am either. They ask me if I'm Chinese. Call me Japanese. Ask me if I know karate or if I can speak kung fu. But at least they know I'm Asian. They can't figure out what she is, so they're always saying something stupid and hurting her feelings."

I look at Ja'nae and Zora, sitting close and laughing 'bout something. "Is it better to be a hundred percent something, or half and half, like Mai?"

Su-bok looks at me like I lost my mind. "It's just better to be you," she says, holding her nose and picking up a box of my old shoes.

# CHAPTER THIRTY-FIVE

I TOLD MOMMA ABOUT DADDY TODAY. How I brought him to our old place after the cops hit him. But I didn't say the part about all us going to the park looking for him. I waited for her to get mad. She didn't. She just put some more home fries on my plate and squeezed ketchup on top of my eggs. Then she said she'd talk to me about it later.

It's almost suppertime now, and Momma still ain't mentioned our talk from this morning. We sitting on the front porch swing—that Dr. Mitchell gave us—watching people working in their yards, or walking their dogs. Momma's toes pat the porch and push us off again when the swing slows down. She says she heard me the last few nights, tossing and turning for hours. She wanna know if that's 'cause we only been in our new place a week, or 'cause my mind is busy with things a girl my age shouldn't have to worry 'bout.

"I'm fine," I say, keeping my mouth shut about the dreams I have at night. Crazy ones, with Zora, Miz Evelyn, and Daddy all coming at me with their hands out. "You think I'm like him, Momma?"

She stops the swing from moving. But doesn't say a word. I put my legs across hers. "He don't care how he treat people, Momma. No matter how good they are to him." Momma changes the subject. Asks me what's going on between me and Zora. I can't look her in the eyes. So I put my feet back on the ground and push. "Nothing," I say.

She asks if this thing between Zora and me got anything to do with money. My eyes get big.

She stops the swing, and cuts the porch light on, 'cause it's dark out now. "Did you borrow and not pay her back, or take what wasn't yours?"

I stand up, and the swing almost tips Momma over. "Sorry."

Momma's mind won't stay put. Now she's talking 'bout Daddy again. Saying how the dope makes him not care for nobody but hisself. "When he's on it, he'll steal the shoes off your feet, or the light out your eye."

I think about him stealing her fur coat long ago, and taking money off me. *How you do that to people you know?* I think to myself. But I done it. To Zora and Miz Evelyn, so it's easy, I guess.

Momma holds my chin, while she stares into my eyes and tells me that I got Daddy's freckles and hair, but I ain't exactly like him. "Not yet." When she says them last two words, she stares extra hard at me. Like maybe she's trying to see if I'm more like Daddy than she knows. "Answer me," she says, pressing hard on my chin. "Did you take money from Zora?"

My eyes look at Momma's smooth, pretty brown skin. They move over her long eyelashes and thick, red lips. "No. Zora's just jealous 'cause she don't want me and you 'round Dr. Mitchell."

I can tell that Momma don't believe me. Every word she's saying now is louder than the one before. By the time she's done telling me that we starting fresh here—"Not dragging our old ways with us like burnt pots that need to be trashed"—the woman next door is up on her feet, looking down her nose at us.

Momma asks me again what I did to Zora. I wanna

ask her how come she cares so much about Zora and ain't worried 'bout me? Then she leans over and picks a ladybug out my hair.

"Nothing bad ever happens to Zora."

Momma blows and the ladybug flies away.

"Daddy steals off me and don't have no shoes, and Zora gets to go to London."

The moon is out now. It's full and clear and shining so bright it feels like God's pointing a flashlight at me.

"Do you want something bad to happen to Zora?" Momma asks.

I think a minute. Then I say what I really want to say. "Sometimes. Sometimes I wish . . . bad stuff would happen to her . . . just so she wouldn't . . ."

Momma finishes my sentence. "Have it so good?"

I catch the ladybug with my hand. "No. Yeah, I guess."

Momma reminds me that if bad things happen to Zora, they happen to Dr. Mitchell and Zora's mother, too. Just like when Daddy went on dope and lost his job, it was me and Momma who ended up on the street first.

I tell Momma that I don't want nothing bad to happen to Dr. Mitchell.

"I don't want anything bad to happen to you *or* Zora," she says.

We go to the back of the house. Watch how the moon makes the red roses look orange and the white flowers look lemon yellow. My eyes are closed. I breathe in the sweetness. Momma says her head aches, and just as quick, she tells me that I'm on punishment.

"He made me let him in the house," I say.

She bends down and snaps a dead flower off its stem. And in a voice as soft as the lamb's ear she planted yesterday, she says that she can't trust me no more. That I lie and sneak around like . . .

She don't finish her sentence. I don't look her way. But I hear the hurt in her voice when she says, "You can do better. Shiketa can do better. Your father too. Y'all just have to wanna do better."

I'm waiting for Momma to yell at me. To maybe go back inside and nail up the windows, or run in my room and empty my money out the window like she did when we lived in the projects. She don't move. She smells the flowers and acts like I'm not even here.

# CHAPTER THIRTY-SIX

Momma went looking for Daddy. She found him. In the park. She won't say exactly what happened. Just that he won't be coming 'round me no more. And that I better not go digging him up and bringing him to our new place, neither.

I've been on punishment ever since. I got one week's punishment for letting him in the house in the first place. One week for not telling her about it. And one week for the mess I stirred up with Zora even though Momma still don't know what really happened.

All I been doing is sitting on the porch swing or watching TV. That means no work. No money. No way out. I keep trying to talk Momma into trusting me again. She shakes her head, no. Tells me I gotta earn it back.

*I am not like my father.* I wrote them words fifty times, all along the sides of the bills I got in my room. Then I snuck out to sit on the swing and called up Ja'nae. I asked her what she was doing. Her mother was at the house, so she couldn't talk.

I call Mai next. She's not on punishment, for once. She and Su-bok are going to the mall. "You don't even like her," I say.

"Well, she's leaving in two weeks. Anyhow . . . her being here kept my dad off my case . . . sometimes."

Mai has to go, Su-bok wants to use the phone to call a boy she met. I rip open a giant bag of Cheetos, then lick the yellow crumbs off my fingers and dial Odd Job's number. I want him to ask Momma to let me off punishment. It ain't his business, he says. I ask him if he wants me to clean up his old place—the two apartments Momma never got to.

"Oh. Them."

"The one we left is empty too, right? So you losing money from all three."

Odd Job says that place is rented out. But the other two need cleaning. He'll talk to Momma about letting me help out. "Don't get me in trouble, girl, by doing something you shouldn't."

I promise that I will do what I'm told. Then I

ask if he helped Momma find Daddy. He won't say.

"Was he high?"

"Yes."

I pat my feet and push off into the air. "It's gonna be cold soon."

"Yeah. Three months from now and we'll be shoveling snow."

Hot air blows across my face. I wonder if my father will have shoes by then.

"Raspberry Swirl," Odd Job says. "Everything's gonna be okay."

"I know."

"You know? For real you know? Or you thinking you know something but you don't really know much of nothing?"

I laugh at him being silly. "Sometimes I know. Other times I don't know why I do what I do."

When Odd Job and I are done, I go inside. Hug Momma so hard she says I'm breaking her ribs. "It's okay," she says, flouring my nose with her white fingers. "I have you and you have me. We'll be just fine."

I look at the spot where Shiketa hit Momma. It's all better now. The hair's grown in and you can't tell nothing bad ever happened there. I squeeze Momma again, then go up to my room and pick up the phone while I still got the nerve. I ask Dr. Mitchell to put Zora on the phone. And before she says one word, I start talking. "I took your money . . . for spite. Not because I really needed it."

Zora's trying to get her say, but I cut her off. "I would never hurt you or your dad on purpose. I like him. Better than my own dad, even."

"I know," Zora says. Neither one of us speaks for a long while.

Then, I don't know why, but I also tell Zora about the money I took off Miz Evelyn.

"You never stole before. Not ever."

"My dad—"

"Steals because he's on that stuff. But you . . ."

"I don't know why I took Miz Evelyn's money."

Zora says she's gotta go. But she'll call me right back. I don't think she will. So I hang up the phone and lay down on my bed. Twenty minutes later, though, the phone rings. It's her. I ask why she never told her dad on me.

"He trusts you."

I stare up at the stars on my ceiling.

"Sometimes people never do trust you again when they know you do things like that," she says.

"So," I say. "Why did you want me to tell on myself, then?"

Zora explains, "The money you took off me came from my dad. He gave it to me to buy your mom a gift when she was in the hospital. But since I couldn't find one I liked, he told me to hang on to it. When I found a nice scarf, I saw the money was gone, and I had to use my own. So you stole the money off of me *and* my dad. And basically off your mom, too."

My legs wobble and my mind races.

"I got the money," I say, reaching in my drawer and pulling out cash.

She tells me to keep it. But I don't want it now. It ain't brought me nothing but trouble.

# CHAPTER THIRTY-SEVEN

BEFORE JA'NAE AND ME EVEN KNOCK on Mai's back door, it opens. Mai's got a sandwich in one hand and a mouth full of food. "Let's go," she says, bread crumbs flying. "I don't want them to see me," she says, licking her lips and locking the door. By the time we get to the front of the house, The Cousins are standing on the porch.

"We're going," Su-bok says. She's got on salmon-colored sunglasses. They match her shorts. She and Mai go at it for a while. Then Su-bok says she's gonna tell on Mai if she can't come along. "You're not supposed to leave the house anyway. You're still on punishment for mouthing off."

Ling takes a pinch of Mai's sandwich and sucks on it till it's gone. "Please. We'll be good."

Mai shoves the sandwich into a trash can sitting by the curb for pickup. "Whatever," she says to The Cousins. Then she ignores them for the next few blocks.

Ling starts complaining right away. "My hair itches," she says, pulling on it, like she can take it off.

"Oh, shut up," Su-bok tells her. Then she grabs Ling by the arm, squeezes her between her legs right where we're standing, and starts French braiding her hair.

Ling pushes her away. "Not you. I want Raspberry to do it."

I don't braid all that good. I tell Ling to let Ja'nae do it.

Mai is getting madder and madder, saying this is why she didn't want The Cousins to come. I am getting mad too. It's *hot*. I'm wearing the wrong jean shorts and top and my skin can't hardly breathe.

Ja'nae whispers something into Ling's ear while she braids her hair. Ling laughs. She hugs Ja'nae, and asks her to carry her. We look at Ja'nae like she's stupid when she picks her up.

"I ain't doing that," I tell Ling. "So don't ask me."

Su-bok and Mai say the same thing.

We are headed to my old apartment building. We

gonna start cleaning up the place. We'll just sweep and pick up today, and do the really hard, dirty stuff next weekend. I get fifty percent of what we make. Ja'nae and Mai split the other fifty. We'll give Ling five dollars and a coloring book.

When we get to the apartment building, nobody wants to go inside right away. I do, 'cause I don't want to run into Miz Evelyn. "Y'all ready?" I ask, after we been on the front steps for a while.

Ling's digging in a flowerpot, making pancakes with spit and dirt. Mai's on the top step, staring inside, asking me who moved into our old apartment. Right away my heart drops. *Miracle*, I think. She musta finally gotten kicked out her old place.

I lean over the railing and look in through the window. The lights are on. You can hear reggae music and smell bacon cooking, even though it's lunchtime. I look across the street at Miz Evelyn's place. Then back inside. "Let's go," I say, hoping to sneak in without Miracle knowing.

I unlock the front door and run up the steps. The door to our place flies open. A woman holding a big stick is right behind us. "Y'all better get out of here, 'fore I call the police."

I show her the key. "We working for Odd Job."

She says her name is Carol. She moved in three days ago. "That apartment up there is a mess. I wouldn't clean it for four hundred bucks."

I am the first to go inside. I walk into the kitchen and get pop out the fridge. Odd Job said he'd leave some there for us. Su-bok, Mai, and Ja'nae go from room to room, shaking their heads. Dry leaves and sticks crack under their feet. Empty beer cans with spiders crawling over them are all over the place. The toilet bowl ain't got water in it, just a thick, green ring of mold.

"I—" Ling says, sucking her thumb, "I don't like it here."

Su-bok goes into the kitchen. "The sink's gone. Even the pipes."

Ja'nae gets pop out the fridge. "It smells."

"Like pee," I say.

"Like the house we worked in that time," Ja'nae says, talking 'bout the boardinghouse we cleaned last year.

It takes us three hours to bag the broken glass and cans. To pick up the tree branches and leaves. I want to work another hour. Ja'nae and Su-bok want to leave. Ja'nae's going to the movies with Ming. Su-bok just wants to go home.

"I'm staying," Mai says. "So you take Ling."

Su-bok's not going for that. She tells Mai that she's supposed to be on punishment, not trying to make extra money.

They argue a little, but Mai and me end up with Ling anyhow.

By the time we head out the building, it's five o'clock. We're too tired to walk, so we go up the street and wait for the bus. Mai and me take turns holding Ling. When the bus finally comes, we are so tired we can't hardly lift our legs to get on it. Ling is doing what she did when we first started out—whining and sucking her thumb.

# CHAPTER THIRTY-EIGHT

WE TRY TO TRANSFER BUSES, but the second one never comes. So now we walking the rest of the way to Pecan Landings where me and Mai live. Ling won't walk, so Mai drags her by the arm for five whole blocks. Ling is screaming at the top of her lungs. Nobody cares, though, until Mai stops and gives Ling a good smack on her butt and legs. You'd think she got cut, she's screaming so loud.

We're in front of Gi-Su's Nail Salon. The man sweeping the pavement eyes Mai when Ling kicks and kicks her. "What you do to her?" he asks Mai.

Mai tells him to mind his own business.

He ignores her. Comes over and wipes snot off Ling's face with his fingers. "Little girl. They hurt you?"

Ling nods her head up and down. Tears come. "I wanna go home to my house."

The man speaks to her in Korean. Ling says something about California. He stares at Mai and says, "Who you?"

Mai grabs Ling's hand and pulls. Ling's whole body gets loose, like a shoelace, and falls to the ground. "Don't touch me," she says.

Mai's on her knees, talking to Ling. "Didn't I tell you to come on?"

The man with the broom sweeps at Mai's legs and feet like she's dirt. "You go. 'Fore I call police."

People are standing around, looking and pointing. Someone tells the man he should call the cops.

When Mai picks up Ling and tries to make her stop crying, Ling asks for Su-bok, then her face turns redder and her mouth opens wide. She cries so hard she chokes and coughs. The man tells Mai to put Ling down.

Mai starts to walk away. "Mind your own business."

"Trash. *Ggam doong yi!*" he says, holding the broom up high.

Mai throws Ling into my arms. "Take her!" she says, walking over to him. Her face is wet with sweat.

"I should just . . . I should just," she says, balling up her fist.

I turn Ling's face away and holler Mai's name. Only it's too late.

# CHAPTER THIRTY-NINE

B‍Y THE TIME MAI'S DAD COMES, she's sitting in the back of a police car. Ling is drinking pop and eating candy that one of the cops bought her.

Mr. Kim, the store owner, and a policeman been inside the salon for an hour. Next thing I know, they back outside. A few minutes later, Mai gets out the car.

Mai's dad looks sad. Tired. Like he could go to sleep forever. "Apologize," he says to her.

She looks at her feet. "Sorry."

"Now. In Korean. Like you mean it. . . ."

The police are by the car writing something down.

Mr. Kim is talking fast to Mai now, and speaking Korean to Ling.

Mai shakes her head no. "You don't know what he said to me."

"Apologize."

"But . . ."

"No buts. Apologize."

"He . . ."

Mr. Kim grabs her by the arm, the one with the tattoo on it. "This man. He won't press charges if you just apologize," he says. "So do what I say. Now."

Mai is talking a mile a minute. Stuttering. Saying, "Daddy, but Daddy, you don't . . ."

Her father turns his back to her. He shakes his head and walks away.

Mai runs behind him. "He called me trash. Black trash."

Mr. Kim keeps his back turned to her. He repeats himself. "Apologize." When he turns around, I see tears running down his face. "You too," he says, pointing to the man with the broom.

I don't know what Mai and the man say, 'cause they're speaking in Korean. When they are done, Mr. Kim whispers something in Mai's ear. She shakes her head and says, "No, Daddy. No." He holds her, rocks her from side to side.

"You look in the mirror and all you see is a little

black girl," he says, pushing curls out her eyes. "I see my sister and my mother. People I love, just like you."

Mai points to the store owner and his wife, then to the people all around us. "They don't see what you see, Daddy. All they see is this," she says, pulling at the skin on her arm. "And this," she says, shaking her hair. "And they can't figure out what I am."

Mr. Kim walks over to the curb and sits down. Mai does, too. "Are you part Indian? they ask me. Mexican mixed with a little Chinese fried rice."

Mr. Kim leans over and kisses Mai's neck, then rubs her back.

She leans her head on his shoulder. "Daddy, I'm so tired. . . ."

Ling sits in Mai's lap and plays with her hair.

Mai tells her father that everybody wants her to choose sides. To just be black, or biracial, or Korean. "I did choose," she says. "Only nobody likes the side I picked . . . not the kids at school, or the boys at the mall, not even you."

Mr. Kim stands up and holds out his hand to Mai. We walk to his car, ignoring people staring at us like we aliens. Mai and her dad speak in English and Korean, so I don't know all of what they say. But I like it when he says that the next time someone asks what she is, she should tell 'em that she's Kim Sung-hee's daughter. "Sweet as honey and brown as fresh baked bread."

I like that. So does Ling. She asks Mr. Kim if her skin will be brown like Mai's when she grows up.

He tells her no. "Raspberry and Mai have something extra special in their skin, that makes it look that way."

Ling stares at her arm.

He looks at her through the rearview mirror. "You have something special too. Just not the same thing."

"Lemon mixed with a pinch of vanilla," I tell Ling. "And so does Mr. Kim."

"Hmmm," she says, wiggling in my lap.

"I'm gingersnap," Mai says, looking back at us. "Raspberry's brown sugar mixed with cherry juice."

Ling bends down and licks my arm. "I eat you up," she says, grabbing Mai's arm too. Before we get through three more stoplights, Ling is lying in my lap, asleep.

Mr. Kim breathes in real deep. *"Doori-dul dah doh jal hae yah hae."*

I get close to Mai's ear and ask her what her father said.

Her fingers roll over the tattoo like she can read

it with her hands. "He says that he and I have to do better."

Ling snores all the way to the house. When it's time to get out the car, Mai takes her outta my arms. Them two have the same-shaped ears and lips, I think to myself. Then I sit back in my seat and wait for her dad to take me home.

# CHAPTER FORTY

**S**UMMER'S OVER—ALMOST. In two weeks we'll be back in school. Two days from now Su-bok and Ling will be back home. I'm having a sleepover tonight at my place, to say good-bye to them and to have a little fun before school starts up again.

I invited Zora. She said no. But Mai, Su-bok, Ling, Ming, and Sato are here. The boys can't stay overnight, though.

"Dr. Mitchell," Sato says, sitting next to me in the swing. "How come you always wear the same pants?"

Dr. Mitchell's sitting next to Momma. He laughs. "Not the same pants. The same color pants."

Sato tells Momma she needs to hook Dr. Mitchell up with some different color pants. "Make him hip. Not like . . . you know."

Momma tells Sato that she likes her man just the way he is. We all look at her. "Somebody's getting married," Ja'nae hollers.

Ling, Mai, and Su-bok make the words into a song, and sing 'em over and over again. My eyes stay on Dr. Mitchell. A few minutes later, he takes me by the hand and down the steps. "Help me with the food."

It's almost ten o'clock and we ain't ate yet. The grill is full of half-cooked burgers and chicken wings. A carved-out melon filled with fruit and bowls of pretzels and chips is sitting on the table.

"I didn't want you to hear this from your mom."

My heart skips.

"Zora and I are going on vacation. Just the two of us."

Dr. Mitchell wants to take me and Momma, but since me and Zora still aren't getting along so well, he can't do it. And he doesn't think it's fair to Zora to take me if that'll make her have a bad time.

I slide the spatula under the cheeseburger, right when Dr. Mitchell wraps his arms around me.

"If you tell me what happened, we can make this whole thing right again. And all of us can go on vacation together."

My hands shake.

Sato leans over the railing. "They'd fire you, if you worked at Burger King."

Dr. Mitchell asks him to give us another minute. Then he fans the smoke and looks into my eyes. "A thousand locks won't keep you safe if you let the boogeyman make your bed."

I don't know what he's talking about.

His mother used to say that, he says. It means that you can't feel safe if you keep the things that scare you locked inside. You gotta talk about 'em to let 'em go.

I bite my lip and put three more frozen burgers on the grill. Ten minutes later Dr. Mitchell heads for the gate.

I'm so ready to lie again. But then I think about Mai's dad. How he stands by her no matter what. "I took—I stole Zora's money," I say.

I'm waiting for Dr. Mitchell to tell Momma he don't wanna be bothered with us no more. He clears his throat. "Keep talking."

I'm trying to explain why I stole the money. He asks how I could do something like that. I turn away so I don't have to look at him.

"Can a brother get a chicken wing 'fore he die out here?" Sato says, hollering over at us.

Momma comes in the yard. She looks at us and says maybe we should take a walk. I wait for Dr. Mitchell to say he ain't going nowhere with me. But he's got me by the elbow, leading me through the gate and into his car.

We drive to his house, not talking at all. "I told her I was sorry. But she's still mad, kinda."

He gets out the car and opens my door. "I am so disappointed in you."

I reach in my pocket and hold my money. "I . . ."

Dr. Mitchell says he knows I've been through a lot. But I ain't the only one who's had it hard. So I got a lot of nerve stealing, especially when Momma's out there working every day to give me a good life.

*He don't wanna see us no more*, I think to myself. Then he opens the front door and calls up the stairs for Zora. When she comes down, I pull out thirty dollars and hand it to him right in front of her. "I owe you ten more."

Dr. Mitchell don't want the money. He says he don't want Zora to take it. He wants us to know he's disappointed in both of us. Me, for stealing. And her for not letting him know sooner, so this whole thing coulda been over with.

I point to Zora. "She didn't want you to hate me."

He looks at me, then at her. "You're like a daughter to me. I couldn't hate you, just like I couldn't hate Zora."

I tell Zora again that I'm sorry for stealing from her, and for trying to keep her dad all to myself. I know it's gonna take a while before we're friends again. But I can wait.

Dr. Mitchell wants to head back to our place. Zora still don't wanna go. Her dad doesn't force her. On the way out the door I lay thirty dollars and some change on the coffee table. *Nothing good comes of bad money*, I say to myself. Then I shut the door and follow Dr. Mitchell to his car.

# CHAPTER FORTY-ONE

**B**Y THE TIME WE GET TO MY STREET, three police cars are parked in front of my house. People in pajamas and street clothes are standing on porches and sidewalks. I know why before I even get to our house. Miracle's here.

Momma's sitting on the porch step with Ling in her lap. A policeman is standing over her taking notes. Miracle is by the police car, pointing my way. She's not screaming, like you'd think. Her voice is calm, like maybe she's too tired to go off on people.

She's talking to the police and pointing at Momma. "She owes me money. Three months' back rent."

He asks her if she was renting a place to Momma.

My mother gets loud when she says she doesn't owe Miracle a dime.

"You missed it," Sato says, almost running over to me. "Miracle walked up to your mom, like she was gonna hit her or something."

Su-bok and Mai pull me over by the tree. Miracle came to the house with two other girls, they say, but the girls took off when the police showed up. Miracle's been living on the street ever since she got put out the apartment. She's blaming Momma. Saying she started everything when she got Shiketa put away.

Miracle points to Momma. "She living in this nice house. Working. Why I gotta live in the streets, and her have it so good, when it's her fault what happened to me."

Momma shakes her head and sits Ling in Dr. Mitchell's lap. When she heads Miracle's way, Dr. Mitchell and the rest of us tell her to stay where she is. She keeps walking. Miracle gets loud. More neighbors come outside to see what's going on.

"Miracle!" Momma shouts.

Miracle looks hungry for whatever words Momma's gonna toss her way.

"Don't you dare!" Momma screams, then lowers her voice. "Don't you dare think you have to act like trash, just because you slept in trash last night. You hear me, girl?"

Miracle's weave is gone, and her short, black curls look dusty. Her shoes are run over and her peach shorts set looks grimy. "You don't understand," Miracle shouts. "If it wasn't for Shiketa, I woulda been out in the streets years before now. Most people don't want no fifteen-year-old around, not even parents."

Dr. Mitchell comes over to Momma, holding Ling in his arms. He whispers in her ear, and she walks back over to the porch with him.

I walk over to Momma. Sit down in her lap. Listen to her tell the police that she don't want to press charges. They want her to. They say they can do it, even if she doesn't. "People in Pecan Landings don't want this kind of nonsense going on," one cop says.

I watch their eyes, our neighbors. See them whispering, curling up their lips and talking 'bout us. A woman Momma's color says, "That's why we tried to keep 'em out the first time."

They put Miracle in the backseat of the car, and the police say for everybody to go home. Nobody moves, not till they drive away and another whole hour passes.

Momma's head hurts. It's been a long time since she said it did. Ja'nae's in the bathroom getting her an aspirin. I'm rubbing her neck and Dr. Mitchell's handing her water.

"We ever gonna eat?" Sato asks, patting Couch on the head.

"You had two burgers," Mai tells him.

Ming heads for the backyard. "Any chicken left?"

I look at Momma. Her and me got the same kind of sad in our eyes. 'Cause even though we don't like Miracle, we don't want her living on the streets neither.

When Ling and Su-bok go to the airport, Mr. and Mrs. Kim take Mai and me too. Ling is crying. She wants to stay here. So does Su-bok.

I speak up for them. "Just come back next summer."

Mai looks at me. "Well. Maybe."

Su-bok writes down my phone number and address. She says maybe she can stay with me part of the time. "You and your mom have so much fun."

She's outta her mind, I think.

"But I wish you still had the old apartment. There's cuter boys around there."

Ling's arms go up. "Sato gave me this." She holds up her fingers. She's wearing three plastic bubble gum rings. Blue, green, and red. "He's my boyfriend."

Mai tickles Ling's stomach. "No. He's Raspberry's boyfriend."

Su-bok asks me if that's true. "'Cause if you don't want him, I do. I could call him up sometime."

Mai looks at me like, *See how she really is?*

I say the words even if they not really true. "Yeah, we go together."

Mai's parents say it's time for Ling and Su-bok to go to the boarding area. They have special permission to go with them. Couch is already in cargo. Mai and I have to stay behind. I pick Ling up. "Kisses," I say, sticking out my lips.

She pushes her face into my chest and strangles me with her arms. "I wanna stay . . ."

I try not to cry. "Here," I say, putting a handkerchief full of quarters in her hand. "There's twenty dollars' worth of quarters."

I give Su-bok a pair of earrings that Ja'nae gave me once. "I'd rather have money." She laughs.

Mai and me wave good-bye. "Your cousins were cool," I say, pulling dead skin off my knees.

She looks at the door they just walked through. "Yeah. Not as bad as I figured."

Me and her wait a long time for her dad to get

back. When he does, he asks her if she wants to stay with them next summer.

"No," she says, stepping onto the escalator. "Not by myself. If Raspberry goes, maybe. Or Ming."

Her dad kind of smiles. *"Uh tok hae hae bohjah."*

"What?"

Mai tells me. "He says, 'We'll see what we can do.'"

Mai's parents hold hands and walk to the right of us. Mai and me are walking side by side staring at some cute boy who's staring over at us. "I have to learn some Korean before I go stay with them."

Mai looks down at her tattoo. "Maybe."

"Maybe what? Maybe you gonna teach me?"

She looks at me and smiles. When she does that, she looks just like her dad.

# CHAPTER FORTY-TWO

SCHOOL STARTS MONDAY. Sato says if I wasn't so cheap, I'd be at the mall buying school clothes, or at the movies, not in Odd Job's apartment building, scraping old paint off walls for money.

I shove him. "You're here with me."

He sweeps more paint chips into the dustpan. "You right. I'm here. Odd Job's gonna pay me and your momma's gonna cook me dinner. That's all right."

Momma's in the kitchen washing cabinets. Odd Job's lying on the bathroom floor, putting in sink pipes. Two of his boys are pulling up bedroom rugs, coughing from all the dirt and dust.

With the new car, the new house, and furniture,

Momma's funds are low. So she's finally doing what Odd Job asked her to do last year—helping him get this place together. Only she wasn't gonna do it unless he really took care of business. Plastered. Put in new pipes and rugs. "Made this place look like something decent people want to live in."

Odd Job knows how to fix things. He's just too busy for stuff like that. But Momma told him if he did it up right, she would help him find some real nice people to move in here.

"Like Miracle, huh?" Sato says.

Miracle's in juvey, hanging with Shiketa, I guess. The cops ain't take her there for showing up at our place. She got put in for grabbing some woman's pocketbook when she opened it to give her some spare change.

Odd Job walks into the living room. He wipes black grease off his hands and onto the back of his pants. He downs a glass of ice water and says, "Girls are supposed to be nice and sweet, like Raspberry. Not thugs, like Shiketa and Miracle."

Momma takes up for the two of 'em. "It isn't over for them yet. If they want better, they'll find a way to do better."

Sato moves closer to me. He slides the scraper across the paint fast. Blue paint chips pop off the wall and hit my cheek and nose. His finger touches my face and rubs my stinging nose. "Sorry."

I swallow and try not to look him in the eyes. I do anyhow. "That's okay," I say, licking my lips.

Odd Job's big boots stomp over to me. "You all right?"

Sato steps back.

"I'm okay," I say, getting embarrassed when Momma comes over too. "Dag. He ain't cut me or nothing."

The men in the back room come out for a break. Momma asks if anybody's hungry, then she takes out sandwiches and chips, Kool-Aid and cold beer.

I head for the door. Tell her that I'll be back after I get me some air. Sato's right behind me. I'm glad.

Sato sits down beside me and dribbles water down the back of my shirt. It feels nice and cool. "You miss it? Living 'round here."

I look at the giant sunflowers in front of Miz Evelyn's place and all the flowers the woman from the first floor got in clear plastic containers on the pavement. I close my eyes and breathe in deep. I don't miss Shiketa, I wanna say. Or my father showing up whenever he wanted. But I miss how sweet the flowers smell in this place. And even though Momma moved most of ours to our new house, it ain't the same. There's so many flowers in Pecan Landings that the sweet hurts your nose sometimes.

Sato stares at me. I cover my face with my hand, 'cause I know he's counting my freckles again. He takes my hands away. Leans over and kisses me. His lips taste like coconut. I move closer to him. Watch his long fingers stretch out on the step so an ant can walk across 'em.

"You and Zora talking yet?"

I tell Sato that Zora's on vacation with her dad. She gets back tonight. "She's still mad, I guess."

When Sato twists his hand and lets the ant walk up his arm, I stand up and tell him the whole story about me and Zora.

He looks right at Miz Evelyn's place. "I wouldn't talk to you neither."

I try to get Sato to see why I done what I did. He don't wanna hear it. "You never stole nothing off of nobody, ever?" I ask.

"Not from my friends. My mom and dad neither."

Miz Evelyn's front door opens wide. I stand up

and open the door. I lick my lips to taste the coconut. "I wouldn't do nothing like that again. Never."

Sato runs in front of me and stops. "Everybody does something bad sometimes, I guess."

I look at his lips and eyes right when he changes the subject.

"You wanna be my girlfriend?" he says, not even looking at me.

"What did you say?"

"Go together. You know. Like Ja'nae and Ming."

I know I should make him wait, or something. But I like him, so I don't waste no time telling him yes. "I'll go with you."

He leans over to kiss me, and stops.

"This is hair grease, not lip gloss," he says, pointing to his lips. "My lips was ashy, you know."

I touch his bottom lip, then rub my finger in my hair. "Is it shiny?" I say, trying to be funny.

Momma calls for us. We both run upstairs. I stop. "I wouldn't steal from you."

Sato gives me this funny look. Then says he wouldn't go with a girl who was a real thief.

I feel funny with him saying that.

"You know, a girl who would just steal over and

over again, not somebody like you, who just did it once 'cause she was mad at somebody."

Momma calls us again. Sato steps to the side and lets me go inside first. I think about Odd Job and what he said about boys treating you special. "Thanks," I say, walking into the room.

# CHAPTER FORTY-THREE

**M**E AND **M**OMMA ARE LYING in my bed. Tomorrow's the first day of school and we're practicing getting me up early again. It's six-thirty A.M. Momma's letting me read Shiketa's letter. She finally wrote the whole thing. Dear Shiketa, it says.

> You and I are a lot alike, you know. When I was fourteen, I smoked and drank and hung out in the streets. Then my mother died. A neighbor took me in and showed me that I could do better. Hard times still follow me like flies do an elephant. But I'm not giving up. Don't you, either. You are strong-minded, like me, and willing to work hard. Better's out there, if you want it bad enough.
>
> Mrs. Hill

P.S. I'm still trying to forgive you. It's not so easy, though. Tell Miracle that I said hello. I will write you both again. Promise.

Momma folds the chocolate stationery the letter's written on, ties the satin brown bow over it, and puts it back in the matching envelope. I put my feet on my walls and ask her how come she never told me none of this stuff before.

"I don't like to talk about it. After my mother died, I lived with Odd Job's family and his mom set me on the right road."

I look at her. "You lived with them? I thought Odd Job lived with your family."

Momma says that Odd Job lived with her when she was nine and hard times hit his family. Then when her mom died and her family fell apart, they moved in with Odd Job's family. "Nobody makes it on their own."

I look up at the stars on my ceiling and count. It's like Momma's talking to herself. Saying out loud how Odd Job's mother taught her to sew and cook. "She showed me what it really means to have people look out for you."

Momma picks up the envelope and holds it up to the light like she can see through it. Then changes the subject back to Miracle and Shiketa. She says she was always in Shiketa's business because she could see she was headed for trouble. "And I didn't want it to find her like it found me. 'Cause I knew maybe she wouldn't be so lucky and turn out so well."

I walk over to the window, and watch the woman across the street get in her red BMW. "Let somebody else help her."

Momma's right behind me. "Somebody else can help her. But we can help her too."

She sits the letter on my dresser. "Everybody does something wrong sometimes."

I think about what Sato said. "Daddy did wrong. You gonna forgive him, too?"

Momma heads out my room. I'm following behind. "I'm trying to forgive your father. But I'm not all the way there yet."

We go out on the porch and sit down on the swing. I reach behind Momma and pick up the purple scarf she left out earlier. I tell her that I haven't forgiven him neither. "But I think about him. Wonder if he got on shoes."

Momma pushes and cool air blows my hair when the swing moves back and forth.

"Nobody's perfect," she says, waving at Mrs. Johnson next door. "No place is perfect either." *She's right*, I think, pressing the silky smooth scarf to my cheek.

"Hurry up," Momma says, driving away, even with my door still open. "My chemistry class starts at nine o'clock."

Momma's down the street and around the corner when I ask if she's picking up Zora. She hadn't thought about it. Figured her father would do that.

"Can we?" I ask.

She drives over to Zora's house. I get out the car and knock on the door. Her dad answers. He smiles and winks at me. "Zora. Your ride is here."

Zora comes down the steps zipping her jeans. I hold my hands behind my back so she don't see 'em shaking. I'm scared. She might tell me she don't wanna ride to school with me.

"Hi."

"Hi," she says.

Words spill out my mouth like pop with too many bubbles. "Momma was gonna take me to school by myself but I told her to come by and get you so we could be together if that's what you wanna do 'cause I know you still mad at me. . . ."

"Oh."

Zora picks up her purse, the red one. Puts it over her shoulder and looks at me. "I'm ready," she says, smiling just a little.

We get in the car. I'm in the front and she's in the back. Momma's on the front steps talking to Dr. Mitchell.

"Sato told me you two go together."

I look back at Zora, and tell her everything that happened between me and Sato back at the old place.

"You can't go selling him candy and chips, now that you go with him."

I think about that. "You right."

"You can't take what's not yours, either."

I cross my heart. "I won't."

She stares at me, like she can see a lie in my eyes. But she never did tell her dad or my mom the full truth about what I did. She still must want them to trust in me. Maybe that means someday she just might forgive me.

Momma gets back in the car and drives off. Zora's

quiet all the way to the school. When the car stops, she gets out and walks to the front door by herself. But she don't go inside without me. She waits till I get there. Just like she used to.

# CHAPTER FORTY-FOUR

**I** **SEE HIS FEET FIRST.** They are long and thin, but the bottoms are not black with dirt like the last time.

"Raspberry!" my father says, when I walk up to our place.

We're almost finished with the apartment. Momma and Odd Job are still there. Me and Sato left early. They started sanding the kitchen floor and the dust was getting all over me.

"You want me to call somebody?" Sato asks, staring at my father.

I tell him no. He says hello to my father and sits on the porch swing.

"I don't want nothing," Daddy says. "Just came to say bye."

I sit down next to him. I stare at the boots he got

sitting on his lap and the new blue work pants he's wearing.

"You working?"

He rubs his chin. "Not real work, like your mother do. But I ain't standing on the corner begging for change like usual."

I look at my father real good. His hair's been cut, but not by a real barber. Maybe a friend with good scissors. The ends ain't all the way even. "You still . . ."

"Living in the park?"

I turn away, 'cause I don't want to see his eyes when he talks about the peach tree I smashed.

Daddy's still living in the park. He says he ain't had no luck since he took my money. "Got beat up two times, and somebody smashed my peach tree."

He digs in his pocket and pulls out a seed. He bought another peach the other day and he's gonna plant the seed soon. "I been clean for two whole weeks now," he says, breathing in real deep. "And for the last four days I been getting up early, doing a day's work."

He reaches in his pocket and pulls out some dollar bills. Ten of 'em. "Yesterday, I almost threw all my money down a manhole, just so I wouldn't go buy none of that stuff."

He can tell from my eyes what I'm thinking. So he asks the question I wanna ask. "Did I go buy it? Smoke it up? No," he says, cracking his knuckles. "I walked all night long. Downtown. Chewed my fingernails down so low, a few of 'em still bleeding." He laughs.

Sato rocks the swing and looks my way. I look at the dark rings under my father's pretty eyes. I listen to him tell me he can't stay in the park. If he do, he gonna be on that stuff again. "I'ma stay clean this time."

Mrs. Kelly across the street is staring at Daddy. I almost tell her to mind her own business. But I get up and pull up some flowers. Hand them to Daddy and ask him if he wants something to drink. "But you can't come inside. Sorry."

He says he ain't hungry. That he ain't staying long neither. He just came by to say hi—to tell me he don't know if he gonna beat this thing, but he's gonna try.

"Why?"

Daddy takes an orange dahlia and sticks it behind my ear. "You know Miracle? She lived up the street from you and your mom."

"Yeah."

"I knew her father. We went to school together. He lives in the park, too. He introduced me to her once. When I saw her sleeping in the park a few weeks back, right next to him, it 'bout broke my heart in two."

Sato's listening. His face looks as sad as Daddy's while he's telling the story.

"I kept thinking. Is that how Raspberry's gonna end up one day, sleeping next to me in that park?"

Chill bumps come on my arms.

Daddy stands up. "Miracle's father shoulda done better by her. I shoulda done better by you, too."

I wipe tears from my eyes. "Daddy."

Daddy's finger goes up to his lip. "Shhhh."

"I'm sorry, Daddy."

He tells me I ain't got no reason to be sorry. That I oughta be glad I got a mother who ain't never let me down. "Everybody ain't got that."

Daddy stares up at the sky. He straightens his pants and shirt and says he better be goin' 'fore it gets dark.

"Wait a minute," I say, running into the house, opening the fridge, and getting a peach.

"Here. You can grow two peach trees if you want."

Daddy rubs the peach on his leg and puts it in his pocket. "That's my Raspberry Girl," he says, turning around and walking off.

Sato goes in my house and comes out with a tissue. "Here."

I wipe my eyes and sit down on the steps. I smile at the woman next door waving to me.

"Odd Job might let him live in his place," Sato says.

I look at him. "You think?"

He stands up. "I don't know. Maybe."

He walks down the steps. I stand up, and we both head up the street. "Junkies quit for real, sometimes, don't they?"

Sato puts his arm around my shoulder. "Yeah. If they really want to, they do."

I wipe my face again. "Momma might talk Odd Job into it, if she thinks Daddy's really serious."

Sato says he bets my father's gonna clean his act up. "Get a job and stay off that stuff."

I stop walking. "I gotta see this lady when we get back to my old street. I got something of hers." I dig in my pocket and pull out a twenty-dollar bill. *I am not like my father*, it says, on all four edges.

We walk awhile not talking or touching. Then Sato points up the street at a fireplug spitting water everywhere. "The water's on."

I take off my sneakers. He does too. I plait my hair

in one, long braid. "Ready?" I ask, holding on to his hand real tight.

"Ready," he says, smiling.

We walk barefooted in the water running along the side of the curb. I look at my feet. They are just like my father's—long and flat.

"Here we go," Sato says.

My heart beats faster and faster. Then the two of us run into the waterfall laughing. Still holding hands when the water rushes at us and takes our breath away.

# Praise for SHARON G. FLAKE

### THE SKIN I'M IN
Winner of the Coretta Scott King / John Steptoe Award
for New Talent

New York Public Library Top Ten Books
for the Teen Age

★ "Flake's debut novel will hit home."
—*Publishers Weekly* (starred review)

### BANG!
ALA Best Books for Young Adults

*VOYA* Top Shelf Fiction

"Disturbing, thought-provoking."
—*School Library Journal*

### WHO AM I WITHOUT HIM?
Coretta Scott King Author Honor Book

★ "Honest and valuable."
—*Kirkus Reviews* (starred review)

★ "Hilarious and anguished, these twelve
short stories . . . speak with rare truth."
—*Booklist* (starred review)

*YOU DON'T EVEN KNOW ME*
The companion to *Who Am I Without Him?*

"These complex and thought-provoking stories
won't disappoint."
—*School Library Journal*

"The immediate voices . . . are well-suited for readers'
theater and for sharing everywhere."
—*Booklist*


**MONEY HUNGRY**
Coretta Scott King Author Honor Book

*Los Angeles Times* Recommended Book for Teens

★ "Razor-sharp dialogue . . . a story that's immediate,
vivid, and unsensationalized."
—*Booklist* (starred review)


*BEGGING FOR CHANGE*
The sequel to *Money Hungry*

An ALA Quick Pick

A *Bulletin* Blue Ribbon Book

★ "Flake's charged, infectious dialogue will sweep readers
through the first-person story . . . Hopeful."
—*Booklist* (starred review)

**Sharon G. Flake's** breakout novel, *The Skin I'm In*, established her as a favorite among middle and high school students, parents, and educators worldwide. She has spoken to more than two hundred thousand young people, and hugged nearly as many. Her work—nine novels, numerous short stories, plays, and a picture book entitled *You Are Not a Cat*—has been translated into multiple languages, including French, Korean, and Portuguese. She is the recipient of numerous awards, such as the Coretta Scott King Honor and the YWCA Racial Justice Award, and her books have been named to many prestigious lists, including *Kirkus Reviews'* Top Ten Books of the Year, Best Books for Young Adults by the American Library Association, Top Ten Books for the Teen Age by the New York Public Library, Top Twenty Recommended Books to Read by the Texas Library Association, and *Booklist* Editor's Choice, among others. She lives in Pittsburgh, Pennsylvania. For more information, go to sharongflake.com, or follow her on Twitter @sharonflake.